Two Friends in Marriage

Weddings with the Moks, Book 3

Jackie Lau

First edition: February 2025

ISBN 978-1-989610-44-2 (ebook)

ISBN 978-1-989610-45-9 (paperback)

Editor: Ali Williams

Cover Design: Sarah Kil Creative Studio

Prologue

Evan

A few years earlier...

"How are you doing?" Jane Yin asks. The video cuts out for a moment, but then her face is back on my computer screen. She's wearing a gray T-shirt, her damp hair loose.

I rub my eyes as I debate how to answer. She's genuinely asking, not just saying it as a greeting.

"I'm better," I reply at last, and it's not a lie. It also doesn't say a hell of a lot because the past few weeks have been not good, to put it mildly. We're in the middle of a pandemic. Outside of the essentials, the province has mostly shut down.

And I'm pretty sure I had COVID-19.

I got sick at the beginning of March, before a state of emergency was declared in Ontario, and at first, I assumed it was a cold. Most of the COVID-19 cases I'd heard of? They involved people who'd recently traveled, and I hadn't been gone anywhere. Besides, I wasn't all that sick. Yet I stayed home out of an abundance of caution, and I'm glad I did. Although I didn't have any acute symptoms, I still don't feel quite right, and it's been a month.

"I'm tired," I say. "It's a different sort of tiredness—hard to explain—but I'm slowly improving. Thank you for the groceries and toilet paper."

"It was the last package. I nearly had to fight someone for it."

The package was open by the time it arrived at my door. Jane had taken half of the rolls for herself before giving the rest to me.

"Next week, I'll do the shopping myself," I say. "I can't imagine I'm contagious anymore, right?" Though it feels like the information on the disease keeps changing. It's just so new. "I'll fashion myself a mask out of...something."

Jane holds up her mask, made from an old shirt and hair elastics.

"Very cool," I tell her.

There's a rather awkward silence.

Normally, I'd fill it, but I'm just not *on*. Aside from going out on my balcony, I haven't left my apartment in four weeks. I miss seeing people, and I'm not used to socializing only on Zoom. That, combined with being sick—and the fact that my girlfriend broke up with me in February—is putting a damper on my mood.

"I'm envious of people who don't live alone," I say. "Some men are complaining about how they have to spend all day with their wife and kids, but that sounds better than being by myself." I punctuate this with a smile so it doesn't sound like I'm whining...too much.

I don't want to bring people down; I'm very conscious of my mood around others, especially now that my depression is getting worse.

"Although, if I lived with someone, I probably would have gotten them sick," I add. "Better this way, I guess, but it would be nice to have the company now."

Jane takes a healthy sip from her glass.

"What are you drinking?" I ask.

"Vodka and grapefruit seltzer." She shrugs. "It's what I had. I thought drinking while on Zoom was better than drinking alone, although if you—"

"No, no," I rush to say. "You're welcome to drink while talking to me."

I'm reminded of an article I saw the other day about a distillery that has switched to making hand sanitizer. The world has turned upside down.

She has another sip. "I wish I didn't live alone, either."

"Yeah?" I've known Jane since our first year of university, which was more than a decade ago, and she's always liked her space.

"Well, if I had someone else in this five-hundred-square-foot apartment? God, no." She wrinkles her nose. "But it would be nice to share a house in the suburbs. To eat dinner and watch movies with someone in the evening."

"And bake bread? I hear that stores are running out of flour."

"They are," Jane confirms. "There was only whole wheat at the grocery store today." She pauses. "I don't want to make bread or pies or whatever people are doing, though I'd be happy to do the eating if someone else was baking. Now that you're feeling better and shouldn't be contagious, you could live with your parents for a bit?"

"True. Might do that."

It's not an option for Jane, though—and not just because her dad lives on the other side of the country.

She drums her fingers on the desk. "It's a pity we're not married and living in a house in the suburbs together. With both of our salaries, we might even be able to buy something."

"Two people don't need to get married to live together."

"But if I'm going to buy property with another person, I'd want some kind of commitment, and since I don't see any romance in my future..."

"No?" I say. We haven't talked about Jane's love life in a long time.

"Dating is such a minefield, and how am I going to meet anyone on an app? How can I swipe left or right when I have no idea who I might eventually find attractive, once I know them better? Plus, there's the pandemic."

"Yeah, it's kind of rough."

"Maybe it's the vodka talking, but I wish I could have an arranged marriage. Even though I literally haven't had a relationship in five years, I think I'd like to get married, and that sounds so much simpler."

"I guess your dad wouldn't—"

"Ha!"

"You could arrange it yourself," I suggest.

"Who would go for that? Would you?"

It's certainly not what I imagined for myself. But relationships haven't worked out well for me, have they? I'm tired of getting my heart broken.

I can't give up hope, though. Not yet.

An acquaintance once said it should be easier for me to find someone because I'm not limited by gender, but it's not that simple.

"In three years," I say, "if neither of us has found anyone, we can have a small wedding and buy that house in the suburbs." I'm not sure how serious I'm being. Everything is kind of weird these days.

"What about kids?" she asks. "I'd like one or two."

I nod. "Sounds good."

"But I, uh, won't want to have sex, except for procreation purposes. Or we could have kids another way. You could sleep with other people, as long as it's fairly discreet. I don't want friends coming up to me and telling me that my husband is having an affair."

It's strange—in a nice way—how matter-of-fact this is. In my last relationship, we still hadn't had a discussion about children by the six-month mark, and the idea of bringing it up made me anxious. But ultimately, that had nothing to do with why the relationship ended.

While not having sex in a marriage might not be my ideal situation, this does sound appealing. I mean, I know we get along—and for long periods of time, too. There are some friends I enjoy in small doses but nothing more. Jane, however, has traveled to Europe with me, and we weren't about to murder each other at the end.

"That's fine," I say.

"I thought you were too much of a romantic to go for this." She taps her finger against her chin. "Let's make it more than three years. How about if we're both still single by my thirty-third birthday, we'll get engaged?"

About three and a half years, then. Her birthday is in early December.

I hold out my hand, my pointer finger touching the screen, and she holds out hers. We pretend to shake on it.

"Do you think handshakes will ever come back," she says, "after this is all over?"

"I don't know, but surely the pandemic won't last beyond the end of the year, right?"

Chapter 1

Jane

It's here. The day I thought might never come.

My thirty-third birthday.

It's not like I expected to die young, but there's some small part of me that couldn't fathom living to be thirty-three when my mom didn't make it to this age. How can I be older than she ever was?

It seems impossible, yet it's now reality.

As I get ready for the workday, my thoughts drift to the spring of 2020. When we were more or less locked down, Evan Mok and I made a marriage pact. I was a little drunk, and somehow, it just made sense. We even shook on it, as best we could.

I didn't expect anything to come of it. I figured Evan—who's objectively more lovable than I am—would be in another long-term relationship by this point. When he started dating Graham a year ago, I assumed this was it.

I was more disappointed than I ought to have been.

I knew I should be glad that my friend was happily in love. It's not like I'm in love with Evan; I've known him for fifteen years, and in all that time, I've never had a crush on him. But marrying a friend really does seem like a solid plan. Dating is far too painful, yet for some reason, I've always secretly thought I'd get married. And it's *not* because I have some old-fashioned notion that this is what you do if you're a woman.

No, I just like the idea of long-term companionship and commitment, and nothing made it clearer to me than the well of loneliness that consumed me early in the pandemic.

I'm tired of being alone.

So, after Evan and his boyfriend broke up, I start thinking more about that Zoom call. In October, when we were enjoying lunch outside on an unseasonably warm day, I reminded him of our pact. I said I wouldn't hold him to it if he wasn't interested, but…

He was.

For the first time in ages, I felt a flutter in my chest. The kind of flutter that people normally associate with romance, but that wasn't the reason; it was just the thrill of taking my life into my own hands. Making things happen, rather than waiting for them to happen to me.

Yes, I'm getting engaged tonight.

Evan sets the bakery box on my kitchen table and lifts the lid with a flourish.

"You didn't!" I say, laughing.

"I most certainly did."

Inside the box is a small cake with "Will you marry me?" written in chocolate.

"Yes," I say, "I most certainly will."

There's no ring—I told him that I didn't want an engagement ring—and no kiss. Kissing on the lips is against our rules. I said I'd appreciate casual touches, like the sort we already do, and perhaps cuddling during movies, but nothing more.

Evan leans forward and envelops me in a hug, one that lasts a little longer than our usual hugs. Then he pulls back. "I guess we should eat dinner before we dig into the cake."

I nod and help him set out the containers of food from my favorite Thai restaurant. I'm about to start serving myself when my phone buzzes. I pick it up, feeling a foolish burst of hope.

An unknown number.

I put the phone aside, annoyed with myself for even looking.

As we start eating, Evan turns to practical matters. "When should we tell our families?"

"I was planning to tell them when I'm in Calgary." It can be such a hassle to fly at Christmas, so I don't always go, but I'm going this year for four nights.

"Okay. I'll do it then, too."

The last time I was in a relationship, our interactions were rather combative, especially near the end. It was exhausting.

But I can't see that ever happening with Evan.

Marriage might not always be smooth sailing, but I think this will give me what I want.

As soon as dessert is over, Peyton and Kaden pull out their phones.

That's fine. They don't need to be paying close attention when I make my announcement. It's not important news to them.

Evan is telling his family tomorrow, but I'm doing it on Christmas Eve, my first full day with my family in Calgary. Outside, it's dark and miserable, but in here, it's warm...though I can't say it's particularly cozy.

"I have something to tell you." I look around the table at my father, my stepmother, and my teenage half-siblings.

My stepmother gestures for me to continue.

I've always called her Suzanne. Nobody has ever tried to make me call her anything else, which I appreciated. Nobody has ever expected us to be close. But maybe if we'd been closer, my dad wouldn't have forgotten about me. He would have seen me as part of his new family, rather than an inconvenient reminder.

I don't know. Our relationship had started disintegrating before then.

I take a deep breath. "I'm engaged."

"Congratulations," Suzanne says, and my father echoes her a moment later.

Kaden looks up from his phone. "You're not wearing a ring."

Peyton rolls her eyes. "You don't *need* a ring. When men get engaged, they aren't expected to walk around with a symbol that they're taken, but women are?"

This morphs into an argument about something else, but then Suzanne says, "Not now," accompanied by a meaningful look, and Kaden returns to his phone.

"Congrats," Peyton says to me. "When are you getting married?"

"This summer," I reply.

Peyton is in her last year of high school. When she was born—before the move to Calgary—I was a year younger than she is now, and I wasn't particularly interested in having a baby sister. As with Suzanne, we get along well enough, but I don't feel like we're *family*. I'm the outsider here, the one who doesn't belong.

"Who's the man?" my father asks.

"His name's Evan," I say. "I've known him since university, but we only started dating this past summer."

My father nods, his face impassive.

There are no comments about how I never told them I was seeing someone, how could I be in a relationship without them knowing? I'm not disappointed; it's what I expected, even if it's accompanied with a blank feeling that matches my father's expression. After all, I've only talked to my father twice in the past six months. He didn't even call or text on my birthday, which wasn't a surprise—he never does. Yet a part of me had still hoped, especially since it was a rather significant birthday for me.

Evan and I discussed what to tell people, and we agreed to pretend we've been dating for a little while—not too long, though, because he and Graham broke up in June. Easier to pretend we've been in a relationship than to explain the situation to everyone. Where we live, young people don't usually get married because they've given up on finding romantic love and don't want to be lonely.

And I wouldn't get married *just* so I didn't have to be alone. Better to be single than to tie yourself to the wrong person, but Evan and I are good friends, and I've thought about this rationally.

After we get up from the table, my father beckons me to his office, which is on the first floor. My family has lived in this house since they moved out west when I was eighteen. I know it well, but it will never feel like home to me, unlike the house we shared with my mother.

My father sits down at his desk and writes me a check.

A large postdated check.

I don't have a checkbook, but my dad is old-fashioned in some ways. Peyton likes to tease him about it.

"For your wedding—or a down payment," he says. "It's dated for January because I need to make sure I have the money in the right account."

I nod. "Thank you, Dad. This is very generous."

And not unexpected, to be honest. My dad and I might not be close—not like we once were—but he paid for most of my schooling and gives me money every Christmas. It's the only way he shows that he cares about me now. I feel like an obligation.

I put the check in my wallet, then help Suzanne in the kitchen. When we're finished, I tell her that I'm going for a walk, and she seems a little puzzled as to why I'd willingly go out in this weather, but she doesn't ask.

I head down the driveway, and the sting of the cold wind on my cheeks is a nice change. Inside that house, I just go through the motions. I'm not really myself.

I wonder when I'll come back here for Christmas again. Maybe never. Evan will want to spend the holidays with his family, and to be honest, I'm looking forward to it. Some people dread dealing with in-laws, and I harbor no illusions that we'll be super close. But I look forward to having family of some kind in the Toronto area, a mother-in-law and father-in-law who will occasionally invite us for dinner.

I met his whole family once, many years ago. It was my second year of university, and my family had just moved to Calgary. I wasn't going to fly out for Thanksgiving; I planned to stay at school. But then Evan asked if I'd want to come to Toronto with him.

So this is what it's like, I thought as we stepped inside and Evan hugged his father. I was an outsider in that situation, too, but I didn't mind. I enjoyed seeing him with his loved ones, and

I didn't feel the need to shut down emotionally so I didn't get hurt.

I assume that tomorrow, when he tells his family about our engagement, it'll be very different from when I told mine.

Chapter 2

Evan

"I'M GETTING MARRIED."

A little nervous about this announcement, I look around at my family. They all ignore their plates of pie and cookies at my news. My parents and my three brothers are here, and Max and Leo have also brought their significant others.

"Yeah, that's a funny one," Jon, my youngest brother, says with a laugh.

Leo shoves his shoulder.

And then there are several seconds of silence.

"*Who* are you marrying?" Mom asks at last.

I hesitate. "Remember Jane, my friend from university?" I continue on, telling my family that we've been dating for several months, and while I'd typically tell everyone by the three-month mark, I'd been burned so many times in the past that I kept it a secret longer than usual. But somehow, everything with Jane just clicked.

I've been in love before. I know how to act the part.

Some members of my family seem suspicious, however. Or they're still stunned by my unexpected news. But then my dad stands up and gives me a hug, and this is followed by congratulations and questions about the wedding.

"When will you get married?" Dad asks.

"This summer," I say. "July, maybe?"

Mom clucks her tongue. "Everything will already be booked up."

Yvonne, Leo's girlfriend, nods. After all, she's experienced in the wedding-planning business: she got to the altar with my cousin back in August...and then she bolted.

Yes, my brother is now dating our cousin's ex.

"We're just having a small outdoor wedding," I say. Jane and I agreed that we'd rather spend money on a house than a wedding. She'd be content to go to City Hall with two witnesses, but I want a little more than that, and I offered to do most of the planning. "Maybe on a Sunday afternoon, since most people are in Toronto." Though a few will be coming from out of town.

"How did you propose?" Dad asks. "Or did she propose?"

I pull out my phone and show them pictures of the cake, which gets a few chuckles. Then I go back to my neglected pecan pie and gingerbread, although none of it tastes as good as it should. I still feel rather anxious.

At the end of the evening, once all the presents have been opened, Max and Kim leave, followed by Leo and Yvonne. When I head out to my car, my mom comes with me. She reaches for my arm after I've put the food and gifts in my trunk.

"Is Jane pregnant?" she asks.

"What?" I yelp. Foolishly, I wasn't prepared for this situation. But an unexpected engagement to a woman...

"I didn't think so, since you aren't getting married until the summer, but I thought I'd check."

"Uh, no," I say, a little calmer now. "Nobody is pregnant. I know it's fast, but we're ready to settle down."

Mom nods. It's hard to tell if she's buying it. "You'll bring her over soon, yes? It must be sad to spend Christmas apart."

"I will."

As I drive home, I wonder what would have happened if I'd told them the truth. I think they would have worried about me, but I suspect some of them are already worrying.

Some parents would just be happy to know their thirty-three-year-old son was getting married, no matter the specifics, but my parents aren't like that. If I'd told them that I'd given up on love, Dad would say I'm too young for such thoughts.

Maybe someone would tell me that the pessimism is just my depression talking. Leo and Max were single for a long time, after all, and look at them now. They both managed to find someone, didn't they?

Actually, my depression isn't terrible these days, unlike a year ago. I finally found a medication that works for me, and sure, I don't like the side effects, but I no longer feel so damn *heavy* all the time. It's definitely an improvement.

Though sometimes, there's still the self-loathing.

I feel like I shouldn't have given up, but at the same time, I'm looking forward to our marriage. It's not what I thought I'd have at this point in my life, but it'll be good...won't it?

And in a way, our marriage pact helped me *not* give up when I was at my lowest. It was something to hold on to when the future seemed hopeless.

When I get home, I check my phone and see a text from Jane, asking how it went with my family. Rather than texting back, I sit down on my couch and call her.

"Merry Christmas," I say when her face appears on the small screen. I might not be in love with her, but the sight of her does make me smile; it's not forced.

"So, what did they think?" she asks.

"They were a little surprised, as expected. Jon thought I was joking at first. Maybe I should have worked harder at easing them into it. Told them we were dating a month ago, or something like that. My mom asked if you're pregnant."

"*What?*"

"Yeah, that was my response."

"I haven't even had sex in almost nine years," she mutters. She's not complaining about a dry spell; it's just a statement of fact. "My family wasn't suspicious or surprised, and nobody asked about pregnancy." She pauses. "I'm a little envious. Your family knows you well enough to actually be surprised. My dad's just like, congrats, here's a check."

"Jane…"

She scrubs a hand over her face. "Actually, you should know…"

My heart thumps loudly in my chest. "Yes?"

"Part of the reason I want to marry you is because of your family."

That hadn't occurred to me, but as soon as she says it, it makes sense. And it doesn't bother me—after all, I'm not in love with her, plus I know my family isn't the only reason we're doing this.

"Don't worry," she rushes. "It's not like I'll expect much of them. But it was nice when I came to your Thanksgiving, and I think it'll be nice to have somewhere to go for holidays."

I feel a smidge of guilt. I should have invited her along more often in the past. Though on many holidays, I had a partner of my own, and it would have seemed weird to show up with both a friend and a partner.

"If we do have kids," she says, "I'll appreciate them having relatives nearby."

We've agreed not to seriously start planning for children until we've been married for a year. We want to be sure the marriage is going the way we hope it will.

And we still have a lot to figure out.

Jane and I are both off work between Christmas and New Year's, and we take advantage of the break to discuss our wedding and marriage plans. She comes over to my place on the afternoon of the twenty-ninth. After eating takeout sushi, we sit down on the couch with her laptop, and she pulls up the document that we started last month.

Now that I've told my family, this engagement feels real in a way it didn't before, especially when we're discussing stuff like wedding venues...and getting preapproved for a mortgage...and where, exactly, we want to live. Frank discussions about finances certainly make things feel very, very real.

Jane freezes in the middle of typing.

"What is it?" I ask.

"I just thought of something. Two things, actually. First of all, I don't usually wear a bra when I'm home, and I have to know you'll be okay with that."

I'm thrown by the change in conversation, but it's not a big deal to me.

"Of course," I say.

"And second of all...I guess we'll have to kiss. When we get married, if nothing else."

"Is that a legal requirement? I assume not."

Rather than replying, Jane starts googling, and a few minutes of research convince us that kissing your spouse is not actually required.

"We can tell the officiant not to say that line," I say. "No big deal." Except it might make my family suspicious that something is up.

If they don't believe I'm in love, will they think Jane is using me in some way?

"We should kiss." She nods decisively. "I mean, unless it makes *you* uncomfortable—"

"No, no," I assure her, "but we should practice beforehand. To make sure it goes okay."

"Good thinking." She sets aside her laptop, cracks her knuckles, and shifts toward me.

I chuckle. "I didn't mean *now*. I meant the day before or something."

"We might as well start now, just in case. It's been years since I kissed someone, and I could be horribly out of practice. Besides, there could be another occasion when we need to kiss to convince people of our relationship."

I raise an eyebrow.

"What?" she says. "It happens all the time in dramas."

"I wasn't aware you watched such things."

She shrugs before shifting even closer so that our thighs are touching. She turns her head toward me and rests her forehead against mine. "This is weird. But yes, I'm sure I want to try."

I tilt my head. As my mouth drops to hers, I have the sudden thought that maybe, this kiss will change everything. Maybe it will show me that I want her as something other than a good friend. Maybe it will make me see her in a whole different light—and vice versa.

Again, the sort of thing that happens in dramas.

But not in real life. Because when her lips meet mine, there's no magic. No zing. It's not unpleasant, but it doesn't make my body flare with passion. I feel strangely distant from it all.

And disappointed, even though I knew this would be a marriage of convenience.

"That wasn't so bad," she says.

"Yeah." I swallow. "Not so bad."

I excuse myself to use the washroom, and when I return to the couch, Jane is typing. I rest my arm on her shoulders, and she doesn't flinch at this casual contact. It's comfortable, yet I feel an ache, a longing for something more. Not with her, in particular, but with someone.

Except I've started more than half a dozen relationships, with a variety of people, thinking that this will be the one. This is it; this is what I've been waiting for.

I know what it's like to be immensely fond of someone's smile or forearms. I know what it's like to sink into a person's body and never want to leave, to be set aflutter by a fingertip touching my cheek.

But my relationships never last, for one reason or another. And after so many times of doing the same thing over and over, wouldn't it be silly to keep looking and expect a different outcome next time?

No, this is sensible. It's for the best.

There's just a little part of me that can't help wondering *what if.*

Chapter 3

Jane

IN THE NEXT FEW weeks, Evan and I find a wedding venue and pay a deposit. We'll get married at an event space north of the city, where we can have the entire thing outside. The ceremony will be followed by a light lunch under a big white tent. Nothing too fancy. I confirm the date with my father before we make the payment; he says it's fine. He doesn't ask many questions.

We also tell our friends from university about our upcoming nuptials, during a small gathering at Lana and Camila's apartment. I don't see these people very often, but I enjoy myself when I do, this small group of queer friends that I met in frosh week. At the time, I considered myself an ally, but later, I started thinking...maybe it's more than that.

They're surprised by the news of our relationship and impending marriage. Except for Lana, who says she always knew there was something between us.

Evan and I have a laugh about that afterward.

I feel like a proper adult, now that I'm planning a wedding and preparing to look for a house. It's silly, of course—I've been an adult for a long time, and nobody needs to get married and own property to be an adult. But still.

One Saturday in late January, Evan picks me up at Finch Station—I don't have a car—and drives me to his parents' house.

In my lap, I clutch a tin of cookies that Evan said would be an appropriate gift.

"Are you nervous?" he asks.

I nod, and when we're at a stoplight, he reaches over and touches my knee.

We've been touching each other more lately—in a nonsexual way—and it's nice. I used to be rather touch starved. Not that I would have admitted it out loud, but I was.

"Have you ever met a partner's family before?" he asks.

"Yes, though the first time, it didn't go well. His parents asked me some weird questions because I'm Asian."

"Right. I remember that now."

"The other time…they were lovely."

That's why I stayed in the relationship a little longer than I should have. The pain of losing a family that accepted me so easily? It was worse than the pain of losing someone whose vision for the future was clearly incompatible with mine.

"I hope you think mine are lovely, too," he says, and that's when I realize he's nervous about what *I* think of them. "I'm sure they'll like you, though. They liked you when they met you for Thanksgiving—"

"It's different when I'm a friend versus a fiancée."

"True. But remember, I've brought a bunch of people home to meet my family before. I know how they react to these things."

"I bet I'll like them," I assure him.

Because from what I know of them, I already do.

When I met Evan, back when we were teenagers, he was the first Asian person I knew who was out. I'd assumed that was just at school, but it soon became clear that his parents also knew, and they were fine with it. And the Thanksgiving that I attended, all those years ago, was pleasant.

Though Evan has tried to reassure me, I'm glad he didn't simply tell me *not* to be nervous. I'd find that decidedly unhelpful.

"The only thing that concerns me," he says, "is that they're still unsure what to make of the quick engagement. So just, um, try to act like we're in love."

"Right."

Evan parks on the street, and we walk up to the house. After ringing the doorbell, he reaches for my gloved hand and squeezes it; my other hand grips the cookie tin.

Evan's father answers, his hair much whiter now. He greets his son with a hug, then hesitates. "Jane, yes? You look just as I remembered. Welcome. You should call me Howie."

"It's nice to meet you again," I say, handing him the cookies.

Evan's mother appears and says, "Ah, you shouldn't have," but she seems pleased.

After we take off our outdoor clothes, my fiancé ushers me to the living room, where one of his brothers and a woman are seated on the couch. On the coffee table, there's a platter of cut-up fruit.

"My older brother, Max," Evan says, "as you may remember, and his girlfriend, Kim." His hand is on my back. "This is Jane."

"Congratulations on your engagement," Kim says.

"Thank you," I reply.

Her gaze lowers. I think she's trying to see if I have a ring to admire.

"I didn't want an engagement ring," I explain. "We'll just have wedding bands."

She doesn't have a problem accepting this, and as I sit down on the couch, I can see Evan debating whether to sit next to me or on one of the recliners. With four people on the couch, it'll be a tight squeeze, but he seems to think it's the right thing to do, as my fiancé. I can't say I mind the warmth of him next to me, his hand on my knee like it was in the car.

"What do you do for work, Jane?" Kim asks.

"I'm an accountant. What about you?"

"I'm an engineer, like Max."

Before I can say anything else, two more people enter the room, and Evan smiles and makes the introductions. Leo—who was in his final year of high school when I last saw him—and Yvonne. They're soon followed by Jon, Evan's youngest brother. He was much shorter the first time we met.

I feel slightly overwhelmed by this large family, so unlike my own.

I also can't help noticing that when Leo sits down on a chair and Yvonne sits on his lap, he looks at her like she hangs the stars in the sky. It might not be obvious to everyone—his facial expressions are fairly mild—but still, I can tell.

Meeting Evan's family has made me particularly aware of the fact that we didn't get engaged in the normal way where we live; we didn't fall in love.

No, we're two rather lonely people who made a pact at the beginning of the pandemic.

"Jane?" Evan's mom says near the end of the night. "Can you come here?"

Evan gives me an encouraging squeeze on the shoulder, and I follow Lynne into the kitchen. She hasn't said a lot to me tonight. Evan had told me in advance that his mother is not always a big talker, so I tried not to worry about it. But my worry spikes as I approach. It's the first time tonight that it's been just the two of us.

"You and Evan don't live together, so I'll give you food separately."

"You don't need to…" I begin, though I appreciate this kind of mothering. It's a novelty for me.

Lynne is going to be my mother-in-law, and as I look at her now, I can't help comparing her to what I imagine my mom would be like, if she were still alive.

But the answer is simply: I don't know.

I was only six when my mom died, and I can't fully trust my memories. Plus, twenty or thirty years can really change a person.

"Are you sure you don't want to live together first?" she asks. "It can be useful, to know if you're compatible."

I just stare at her. She's *encouraging* us to live together before marriage? My past experience with Asian mothers did not prepare me for this possibility.

"Well, we might live together first if we buy a house before July," I say. "But we've known each other a long time, even if we haven't dated for long. I'm sure."

I think of Leo and Yvonne and feel a sliver of doubt. Maybe I should have held out for something like that, but it seems unlikely it would have happened.

"The engagement was very surprising," Lynne says.

"Yes, I'm sure it was. But when you know…you know."

I hope that sounds convincing.

She nods. "My engagement was very quick, too."

I'm not sure it would be appropriate to ask about that, so I stand there awkwardly.

"Evan says your family lives in Calgary?"

"Yes," I reply. "My dad, my stepmom, and my half-siblings."

"What about your mother?"

"She's dead."

"Ah, I'm sorry. Evan didn't tell me."

"It's okay. It was many years ago." I curse myself after I say it. This has happened before: when someone says they're sorry, I try to brush it off by saying it's been a long time. But I lost my mother when I was a child, which doesn't exactly make people feel better.

"If you'd like, we can go out to Calgary to meet your family before the wedding."

"No, that's not necessary," I assure her.

"We will all meet at the rehearsal dinner, then? I don't know much about these things because Evan is the first of my sons to get married. But I think here, traditionally, the groom's family pays for the rehearsal dinner? We're more than happy to do that and help with the cost of the wedding."

"Thank you," I say. "I'll discuss it with Evan." I hadn't thought about a rehearsal dinner—is it necessary? Our ceremony will be very simple, and we're using the officiant who married Lana and Camila.

There's an uncomfortable pause, and I wonder if I'm already screwing up this relationship, which is the last thing I want to do.

I'm little relieved when Evan comes into the kitchen.

"There you are." He puts his arm around me and kisses me on the cheek in a way that feels quite natural.

Evan doesn't look much like his mother. Actually, he doesn't look much like his father, either, but he and Max definitely have similar features. They both wear glasses, too.

He turns to me. "Are you ready to go? Did my mom give you enough food?"

♥ · ♥ · ♥ · ♥ · ♥

On the drive back to the subway, Evan asks how I think it went.

"I'm not sure I can do this," I say quietly.

"You don't want to get married anymore?"

"No, no, that's not what I meant. I just...I'm not sure how to be part of a family. And I think your mom finds it weird that we're not living together first before buying a place. For, um, compatibility. I didn't know how to react."

"You did just fine," he says. "My parents occasionally say things that surprise me as well. My dad said he thinks we're good together, and I hadn't expected him to actually say something like that."

I admit I'm rather pleased.

I hesitate before asking my next question. "I'd like to tell Claudia the truth. Is that okay? I'm not sure how I'd convince her of the story we're telling other people anyway. She'll keep it a secret, I promise."

I still haven't told one of my closest friends that I'm engaged, even though it's been almost two months. I've gotten away with it because we don't have any other friends in common—and she lives in B.C. But I can't do that much longer, especially if I want her to come to the wedding.

"Sure," he says. "Whatever you need to do."

"I have some news," I say, looking at Claudia on my laptop. "I'm getting married."

The video suddenly looks weird. I think she spit water on her screen, and I can't help laughing as she rubs it with her sleeve.

Claudia and I first met on an ace-spec forum that no longer exists. Since we live over 3000 km apart, we've only seen each other in person a handful of times. She's white and a couple of years younger than me.

"I'm sorry," she says, "did you say you're getting married?"

"Yeah. To Evan." The two of them met once before.

"I didn't know you were dating."

"We're not." I explain how we made a marriage pact back in 2020, and how I like the idea of settling down. Of constant companionship with a friend. Possibly even having kids. "I feel like I'm taking control of my life."

"What about sex?"

"If we decide to have kids the old-fashioned way, then we'll consummate the marriage, but otherwise, we won't have it."

"He's okay with that?" she asks.

She knows *I'm* okay with it; she knows I haven't had sex in years, a state of affairs that doesn't bother me. I've only ever been attracted to two men—and it's been a long time since I've felt sexual attraction. I do have a libido, but I take care of that myself a few times a month. Sex isn't something I miss, and it's part of what makes dating so complicated for me: I'm never attracted to someone from the beginning, but in a long-term romantic relationship, it *is* something I'd want. At least, I did in the past, though my sample size is small.

And even though it usually takes me a while, I've known Evan for fifteen years, so if it was going to happen, I'd think it would have happened already.

"He's free to get it outside of our marriage. I fully expect him to do that at some point, though he doesn't seem too concerned about it. Don't worry—we talked about all this before we got engaged. Which was, um, in December."

"And you're only telling me now?"

"Sorry. It's a weird situation, and most people don't know the truth."

"You know I'm all about weird situations," she says, and I laugh. "If you think you'll be happy in this sort of marriage, then I support you. When's the wedding?"

"July. You'll be invited, of course. I hope you'll come."

"Definitely! Just give me the date and I'll look at flights."

When Claudia and I end our call, I feel relieved. It was nice to tell someone, other than the person I'm marrying.

But now that it's done, my brain jumps to something else I need to figure out: my wedding dress.

I don't have any female relatives to go dress shopping with me, and Evan and I aren't having a proper wedding party. Once Claudia books her flight to Toronto, I ask if she'll be a witness, and she agrees; Max will be the other one. We tell them that they can wear whatever they want.

"You can wear whatever you want, too," Evan says to me. "It doesn't need to be a white dress—or even a dress."

But although I haven't spent my life dreaming of my wedding, I did always imagine wearing a white dress.

"You could ask Lana and Camila," he suggests, when we're talking on the phone one day. "Or I could go. I think it's supposed to be bad luck for me to see you in the dress before your wedding day, but I'm not worried about that."

I brighten. "Would you?"

I just want something off the rack. No more than $1,500.

We start with a store in Corso Italia, and the sales lady asks me questions about what I want, but I'm not well-versed in the language of dresses. I tell her that I'd like I bit of lace. Nothing strapless. Despite my limited help, she quickly selects four dresses that look promising.

The fit of the first one is all wrong, though, and the second is okay, but not something I'd spend over a thousand dollars on. As I return to the fitting room, my thoughts start to spiral. I know I shouldn't have expected the first or second dress to be perfect, but I fear I'll never find something, and I don't know anything about this sort of thing because I don't have a mom...

I exit the dressing room in the third dress, not feeling terribly hopeful. Some women say they *know* as soon as they put on the dress, and I don't feel that way about this one, either.

But when Evan sees me, he smiles. "I like it. You look very pretty." He turns me to face the full-length mirror and keeps his hands on my lace-covered shoulders. "What do you think?"

"Your fiancé has good taste," the sales lady says.

She doesn't find it weird that my groom-to-be is accompanying me to search for a wedding dress. Even if it's not "tradition-al," she's probably seen everything.

I take a closer look at myself in the mirror, the lacy details on the bodice, the long sleeves. It really is gorgeous. My mind stops racing; I can imagine myself getting married in this one.

I try on a few more dresses, just in case, but in the end, that's the one I buy.

When we leave the store, I'm relieved to have one more thing checked off my list, and I'm also relieved that I don't have to do any of this alone.

Not surprisingly, buying a house is harder than buying a dress.

We get a real estate agent and a preapproval for a mortgage. We tell her what we'd like and start going to viewings. We put in bids for two houses in Markham, but we don't get either of them.

It seems ridiculous that two thirty-three-year-olds, who've both worked for over ten years, have to consider themselves lucky to even have a chance of buying a house in the Toronto suburbs. But I know we're lucky. Our parents aren't giving us six figures for a down payment, but our families paid for the majority of our schooling. Twenty-five years ago, it would have been a given that we could buy a house; unfortunately, prices have skyrocketed.

I knew it might be tough, but I feel like I wasn't fully prepared. I'm doubtful we'll close on a house before July. Maybe it was foolish to think we could plan a wedding and buy property in seven months, even if it's a simple wedding.

One spring day, Evan and I go to an open house in Thorn-hill. It's the smallest, shabbiest house on a nice street, and it's painfully busy.

As we exit, we look at each other and shake our heads. We're not going to put in an offer, and I sigh as I head to Evan's car down the street. I've just put on my seatbelt when my phone rings. It's my father, so I answer.

"Hi, Dad," I say.

"Jane, I'm so sorry."

My heart rate kicks up. "What's wrong? Did something happen to Suzanne or the kids?"

"Ah, no."

"To you?"

"I'm fine, but I can't come to the wedding."

I shouldn't be surprised. My dad has been disappointing me for over two decades; he missed both my high school and university graduations. Yet I assumed he would at least show up for my wedding, even though he has to fly across the country. How silly of me.

"I have to go to Denver for an important meeting," he explains.

It's three months away, though. Shouldn't there be something he could do? Change the date or ask someone else to go instead of him?

But I don't say that.

"I understand." My voice is flat.

On the other end of the phone, my father makes more excuses that sound like gibberish to me. I know that if Peyton or Kaden gets married, he'll be there no matter what.

I don't point that out. I just nod and murmur a few words until he ends the call. Then I set aside the phone and look vacantly out the windshield.

"What's up?" Evan asks.

"He's not coming to the wedding. Business meeting."

"*What?* Do you want me to call back and yell at him? Can't he—"

I hold up a hand. "Don't bother. He's made up his mind."

I appreciate the offer, though, and the idea of Evan yelling makes me chuckle. I've never heard him raise his voice.

He reaches across the console and puts a hand on my shoulder. My eyes suddenly brim with tears, but I don't let them fall. It's not worth crying over my father; I've known that for a long, long time.

I look down at my hands. "I know it's hard to believe, but in the years after my mom died, he really was a good father. It was like the two of us against the world. He never missed an event. He made sure I had therapy. Maybe that doesn't sound remarkable, but I don't know how many fathers in the nineties would have done that for their grieving kids. And then..."

Puberty was simply too much for him. He couldn't handle the fact that I needed bras or pads. He gave me cash and told me to figure it out, which once led to me sobbing in Shoppers until a friend's mom found me. He thought I didn't need him anymore, but I did, just in a different way.

I shake my head, and Evan doesn't press. He leans closer to me and runs his fingers through my hair in a soothing manner.

"Is this okay?" he asks.

"Yeah. It's nice." I can't remember the last time someone touched my hair like this. It's as if he's stroking some of the pain away. Tension leaves my body as I relax against him, and a few tears slide down my cheeks.

"I can't promise I'll never disappoint you," he says. "I wish I could, but I can't. But I'll do my best to always be there when you need me, and if I screw up, just remind me that I promised you."

"Okay," I whisper.

And from then on, I feel like we're truly engaged. We're not sleeping together or exchanging *I love you*s—in fact, no man has ever said that to me before—but our relationship means something.

Chapter 4

Evan

Jane is calling, but I can't pick up because I'm in the middle of a Zoom meeting.

As soon as I can, I call her back.

"We got the house!" she says.

I hadn't let myself be too hopeful when we put in another offer, but I didn't express that out loud. And now, it's finally happened. We're going to own a four-bedroom house in Richmond Hill. It's a little dated, but there's no critical work that needs to be done.

We end up closing on the house less than two weeks before the wedding, and we both get our stuff moved in a few days later, on a Friday. That first night, too tired to cook, we order pizza and eat it at the kitchen table—the one that used to be in my apartment.

"We should buy some patio furniture so we can eat outside," Jane says. "And a barbecue, though maybe we should wait until next summer."

Yeah, we've spent a lot of money lately, and looking at my accounts online makes me cringe. Jane and I also have a joint account now—for paying the mortgage and other household bills—and we've agreed on how much we'll each put in monthly.

I can't believe I have a mortgage.

I used to think I wouldn't want to live north of Steeles, and I hoped to own a condo downtown one day. That was how I saw my future. But in 2020, stuck in a high-rise, I ached to have a yard. I wanted to step outside and see my garden. Even the idea of having a driveway to shovel sounded appealing.

And when the world (sort of) returned to normal, that feeling didn't leave.

After dinner, we meticulously clean up, not wanting a crumb left on the floor or counter of our new house, and then we both do some unpacking in our bedrooms.

From the beginning, we agreed on having separate bedrooms. Of course, that might make some people suspicious of our marriage, but there are definitely couples who maintain separate bedrooms for one reason or another. My mom raised an eyebrow when she was here earlier, but Jane rushed to assure her that she's a finicky sleeper and besides, she snores very loudly. (From traveling with her, I know that's a lie.) Mom told her to participate in a sleep study.

I have the biggest bedroom, which has an en suite. Jane suggested this arrangement if it meant she got a second bedroom for her office; I'll be working in the basement.

I'm hanging up clothes in the walk-in closet when Jane appears at my bedroom door.

"Hey," she says. "I'm going to bed now. I'm beat."

How do goodnights work with a committed friend and roommate? I'm not sure, but I walk toward her and wrap her in my arms. She smells faintly of peaches.

"We did it," I say.

"Yes, we did. See you in the morning."

But as she returns to her bedroom, I no longer feel like I've accomplished something big. No, I feel strangely hollow.

I just bought a house with my soon-to-be spouse. We shouldn't necessarily be having sex right now—after all, it's been a long day, and we're not twenty-two—but I feel like we ought to be snuggling in bed together, even if one of us eventually goes to another room to sleep.

Until we made that pact, I never imagined marriage would be like this.

Same-sex marriage has been legal in Ontario since before I started high school. When I came out at the age of fourteen, it was in a world where I'd be able to marry the person of my choice, no matter their gender. That didn't mean everything was rainbows and unicorns, but I always felt like I had options.

I would get to marry for love.

Yet here I am, nine days away from my wedding, and there's no romance. A friendly sort of love, sure. But not the kind I thought I'd have.

What if I hadn't given up? Sure, the pact might have given me solace at one point, but I didn't need to go through with it. I was dissatisfied with my career and managed to make a change in the fall, rather than assuming I was stuck. Maybe I could have succeeded here as well.

It's not too late, a voice in my head says.

I scoff. It's definitely too late. We own a goddamn house together.

Besides, I made a promise to her, back when her piece-of-shit father said he wasn't coming to our wedding. Aside from the logistical mess, flaking out on that promise is not something I'd do to Jane. I refuse to be another person in her life who thoroughly disappoints her. She doesn't deserve it.

Listlessly, I wash up. There are two sinks in this bathroom, but it seems unnecessary. It's not like there will ever be two people in here at the same time.

I crawl into my queen bed. Though the mattress is familiar, the outside noises are slightly different from what I'm used to, but eventually, I fall asleep.

Alone.

A few days after we learned that Jane's father wouldn't attend the wedding, I broached the subject of the rehearsal dinner, and she said she didn't want one. I also asked if she wanted someone else to walk her down the aisle, and she said no. We'd simply walk together.

When I explained all this over the phone to my mother, she was aghast that Jane's father wouldn't show up. She asked if it was a financial problem, and I assured her it wasn't. Then she asked if there were any other relatives that Jane wanted to be there—from anywhere in the world—and offered to help with the airfare.

But Jane hasn't had any contact with her mom's family since she was a kid, and she has a limited relationship with her uncle and cousin on her father's side. They're in China, and she hasn't seen them in a decade. And I guess her stepmother sees no reason to come if her father won't be there.

So, when we get married today, all of the family guests will be my own.

I'm glad Claudia flew in yesterday for Jane, and I'm happy to have her stay in our guest room—I can't believe we actually have a guest room—for two nights. To be honest, I'm also glad she knows the truth. If she didn't, she'd probably refuse to stay with us tonight.

I head downstairs at seven. Jane is already up, coffee nearly ready.

I'm getting used to my new reality. Living in a house, having a home office that isn't a corner of the living room. Eating dinner with someone else every night. It's nice.

But I continue to have complicated feelings about what we're going to do today, and as I watch her pour a mug of coffee, humming quietly to herself—"Here Comes the Bride," heh—I'm hit with a slightly different thought than the ones I've been having recently. My complicated feelings have been self-centered, but now I think: *She deserves better.*

"Jane," I say.

She turns around, mug in hand. "Hm?"

"Are you sure you want to tie yourself to me?" I gesture feebly. "You deserve to marry someone...who loves you."

She puts down her mug, walks over to me, and sets a hand on my chest. It's warm from the coffee. "You deserve that, too. But we were both tired of not getting what we wanted, and so—have you changed your mind?" Though she speaks evenly, I can tell she's freaked out. We've spent months setting all this up.

I think of Yvonne, who ran up the aisle rather than getting married.

"No," I assure my fiancée. "I just wanted to check that you hadn't."

"Of course not. I'm ready for this."

In an attempt to convince her, I press a quick kiss to her neck—I don't know why I think this will work, but it somehow makes sense—which is how Claudia finds us when she walks downstairs.

"Am I interrupting something?" she asks, waggling her eyebrows.

"No, no," I say. "We're all good."

After breakfast, we get in my car—I need to remember to add Jane to the insurance—and I drive the three of us to a salon. Two people have come in early to assist us. I'm getting neutral makeup, just so my features look a little sharper in the pictures. Jane asked if I wanted something more glamorous—there have been phases in my life when I experimented with dramatic eyeshadow. I appreciated the thought, but I said no.

By ten o'clock, makeup and hair are done: a simple updo for Jane and a blowout for Claudia. After picking up the bridal bouquet, we return to the house, where I put on a tux. Claudia changes into a sleeveless pink dress before assisting Jane with the wedding dress that we picked out all those months ago.

"You look beautiful," I tell my wife-to-be as we wait for the limo, and I'm not lying. She looks lovely. I just wish that said loveliness stirred up stronger feelings in me.

"You're not too bad yourself," she says lightly.

It's an overcast, cool summer's day, which is fine with me. If it were hot and humid, I'd be sweating buckets. The important thing is that it's not supposed to rain until this evening.

It's less than a ten-minute drive to the venue. Although we booked the venue before buying the house, they coincidentally happen to be quite close to one another, which is convenient. My parents are already here, and the photographer takes a few pictures before the other guests start arriving. Jane met most of my extended family at the Lunar New Year, but I introduce her to the few people that weren't there.

Five minutes before the appointed time, we urge everyone to take their seats—"no bride's side and groom's side, sit wherever you like"—and share a few words with the officiant, who stands in front of the chairs set up on the grass. There's a simple flower arch behind them, nowhere near as grand as the décor at the last outdoor wedding I went to (my cousin Mirabel's), but neither

Jane nor I were too concerned about such things. We just didn't want the planning to be too stressful.

When the music begins, I take a deep breath and paste on a smile. I'm not standing next to the love of my life, and it's not how I would have once imagined my wedding day, but this is it, for better or worse.

Jane and I link our arms and proceed down the aisle together. I feel like I'm having an out-of-body experience as the ceremony begins, even as I keep my eyes focused on Jane. Like this can't possibly be me getting married, but someone else, and I say "I do" a split second later than I should.

"You may kiss the bride," the officiant says.

As I lean in, I'm very aware of just how odd the act of kissing is. Lips against lips. Tongue on tongue. (Well, not in this particular kiss, but still.)

But as I pull back and smile at my wife, a wave of fondness overtakes me.

I've made promises to her, and I'll do my best to be a good husband, even if some silly part of me thinks I should have held out for love.

"Congratulations," Auntie Gladys says, pressing one of my hands between both of hers in the receiving line. "You're lucky she didn't run!" She laughs as though this is a funny joke.

My mother, who's standing to my right, glares at her.

But I just say, "Yes, I'm very lucky."

I'm married to Jane, and everyone important to me is here to celebrate. There's something bittersweet about the whole thing, but I will make the most of it.

For her sake, if nothing else.

Chapter 5

Jane

DUE TO MY LACK of family and limited number of friends, I haven't been to a ton of weddings. Perhaps my own wedding would be less overwhelming if I had.

Or maybe not.

"Where are you going for your honeymoon?" asks one of Evan's aunts. I'm pretty sure her name is Doreen, but I'm not entirely certain.

"We're not going on a honeymoon," I say. "The wedding, the new house—it was expensive enough." I'm not great at making casual conversation with people I barely know, but I do my best.

"You don't have to go anywhere fancy. After all, you might end up spending most of your time in the room."

I stiffen—and I don't think that's different from the reaction I'd have if Evan and I were actually sleeping together. It's still a weird thing to hear from his aunt!

"Doreen." Lynne is suddenly at my side. "Don't make her uncomfortable."

She also swooped in to save me from Gladys, who seems unimpressed that we're just having a light lunch, not a full Chinese banquet.

But I can't say I'm disappointed with our simple wedding. About fifty people—half friends, half Evan's family. A little mingling outside after the outdoor ceremony, and in a few minutes, we'll eat under the tent.

Lynne also made a point of mentioning that Gladys is always complaining and I shouldn't take anything she says personally.

I feel a tug on my skirt and look down.

"You're so pretty!" says the little boy. "Like a princess."

"Why thank you, Nolan." I crouch down to speak to him. There are only two children at the wedding: Nolan, the son of Evan's cousin and her wife, plus the baby daughter of two of Evan's friends.

"Are we going to eat soon? I'm hungry."

"Sorry." Isobel—Evan's cousin—jumps in. "Don't worry, he's not starving. He just had Goldfish crackers, but he's excited about the cake."

"I think we'll be eating very soon," I say.

"Can I sit beside you?" Nolan asks.

"No, she's sitting at another table," Isobel says, "but we'll have Auntie Jane and Uncle Evan over for dinner later this summer, okay?" She smiles at me.

Auntie Jane. I've never been anyone's auntie before.

Technically, I'm his mother's cousin's wife, but I'm an adult in this child's life. Of his seven first cousins—five on his dad's side and two on his mom's—Evan is closest to Isobel, so I expect to see Nolan at more than the occasional wedding or holiday.

As Isobel leads him away to clean his hands in preparation for lunch, I think of my absent family. Evan's American relatives flew in for the wedding. Only from Philadelphia, which isn't a long flight, but still. They're here, and my father isn't.

"Hey." Evan touches my shoulder. "How are you? Is my family overwhelming?"

He's wearing a gray tux that I helped him pick out. His tie has become the tiniest bit crooked since the ceremony, and I reach up to fix it.

"No," I say. "Nolan just said I look like a princess."

"You do."

Lana and Camila approach us. Lana is wearing a wide-legged purple jumpsuit—with her long legs, it looks much better on her than it would on me—and Camila is decked out in a blue cocktail dress.

"Hey, you two lovebirds," Lana says. "How does it feel to be married?"

"Good," I say. "Very good."

But I swear Evan's smile slips a fraction of an inch before he wraps his arm around me and echoes my words.

Or perhaps I imagined it.

There's no long head table for lunch: Evan and I are seated at a round table with his parents, his brothers and their girlfriends, and Claudia. We start with a seasonal salad, followed by lemon roasted chicken, and then it's time to cut the wedding cake.

Although Evan and I didn't bother with speeches and dances, we both wanted to have a cake, and we were both in agreement that we cared more about the taste than the appearance. There's no fondant, just swirls of vanilla buttercream with a few artfully placed buttercream flowers. The bottom cake is chocolate; the top cake is vanilla with a raspberry filling.

The cake was wheeled into the tent earlier, and now, I stand up and grab the provided knife. Evan places his left hand over my right hand. It feels strange to cut a cake while someone else is touching me, but I manage to cut a slice of the top cake. He breaks off a tiny piece and holds it to my lips. I open my mouth, and my lips graze his fingers.

Mm.

Feeding each other cake feels rather performative—like our kiss at the end of the ceremony—but I'm happy to do it.

And when someone from the venue starts serving up the cake, I take the first chocolate slice and walk it over to Nolan, and everyone laughs.

By four o'clock, the reception is officially over, and we thank everyone for coming before they head home. Claudia gathers up the guestbook and gifts—nearly all envelopes—and we head home in the limo with the boxed-up cake.

Home.

I'm still getting used to the idea that this house is now *ours*.

In my bedroom, I take off my dress but leave my hair and makeup. When I step into the kitchen, Evan and Claudia are already there, wearing casual clothes. The two of them are taking apart my bouquet and putting the flowers in vases—I'd mentioned that I want to keep the flowers—and they're laughing about something or other.

"What do you think?" He gestures toward a vase with pink and white roses, and I chuckle when he does jazz hands.

"Looks good," I say.

"You hungry? Anyone need more than cake tonight?"

"Actually, I'm a little hungry."

Nobody is in the mood to cook, so we order pizza to our new house for the second time.

After I remove the pins from my hair and wash it—I need to get out all the hairspray—I walk into Evan's bedroom, since the door is open. I'm wearing a loose T-shirt and pajama shorts, no bra, and it feels normal to be around him like this.

Evan is sitting at the end of his bed, and he's also in a T-shirt and shorts. His elbow is resting on his knee, his hand is splayed over his face, and there's something oddly compelling about the pose, the slight crease between his eyebrows. He looks like he's deep in thought. I'm about to return to my room when he looks up at me and smiles. He pats the mattress, and I come to sit beside him.

"We did it," he says.

"Yes, we did."

He puts his arm around me and pulls me against his lean frame, and we sit like that for a moment before he kisses the top of my head.

I'm acutely aware of the fact that this is not how newly-weds are supposed to part on their wedding day. And it doesn't bother me...much. I'm not usually too concerned about what I'm "supposed" to do. But the occasional wistful looks on his face—plus the question he asked me this morning—make me wonder if he had doubts, even if they weren't enough to run back up the aisle.

"You okay?" I ask him.

"Yeah. I'm fine, just a little tired."

If he doesn't want to talk about it, I won't force him. I squeeze his shoulder, then head back to my room and check my phone.

My father didn't even send me a text on my wedding day.

I pick up the framed photo on my dresser, the one that has sat on my dresser for as long as I can remember. It was taken at the Sears photo studio, back when photo studios at department stores were still a thing. Back when Sears still existed in Canada. It's one of the few pictures of me with both my parents. I'm three years old, and apparently, I was Not Happy with the whole experience, but I'm smiling in the picture.

I imagine having my mother—and my father—at my wedding. Going dress shopping with her. Would she have had lots of opinions about the wedding? Would I have told her that I wasn't marrying for love?

Maybe, if my mom were alive, I wouldn't have made a marriage pact with Evan. My life might have turned out very differently. Maybe, for one reason or another, I would have ended up going to another university and never met him.

Maybe I would have met the love of my life instead.

I shake my head at these sentimental thoughts. This is why it's best not to think of such things, but it's hard to entirely avoid it on your wedding day.

The next thing I know, I'm wondering whether I would have been easier to love—and more open to it—if she were still here.

If, if, if.

Some people say that your wedding is the happiest day of your life. But I never expected it to be—and it wasn't.

Still, it went well, and I'm now married to a nice man with lots of family.

Chapter 6

Evan

BOTH JANE AND I have taken the Monday after our wedding off. In the morning, we brave the traffic to drive Claudia to the airport. She playfully threatens me in the drop-off area.

"You better not screw this up," she says, "or I will come for you."

Despite her tone, I don't think she's joking, but that's okay. I intend to be a good husband.

I might feel a bolt of longing when I witness a couple having an emotional goodbye, but then someone behind me honks, and I return to my senses.

That isn't for you. You don't deserve it.

I wince at the thought that pops into my head, unbidden. I didn't get married to my friend because I don't think I deserve love. It just wasn't happening for me, and I wanted companionship and home ownership. So, I did what was practical.

As I get back on the highway, I try to focus on our plans for the day instead. We're going to Canadian Tire to get a bunch of things we need for the house, including a lawn mower. We have a front flower garden and a back vegetable garden, though it's a little late in the year to do a lot with those. But for next year...

"I want bisexual flowers," I say.

"Flowers that produce both sperm and eggs?" Jane asks. "Isn't that what the word means when you come to flowers?"

"Maybe that's true. But I mean flowers that can turn both blue and pink, depending on the soil conditions. Sometimes clusters of them look like the bisexual flag. I forget what they're called. It starts with an *h*."

"Bisexual…flag…flowers," she says. I think she's typing that into her phone, but I can't see because my eyes are focused on the road. "Okay. Yes. It's a type of hydrangea. The color is related to the pH of the soil."

"What do you want in the garden?" I ask.

"Cherry tomatoes and herbs. Maybe daffodils and tulips out front for early spring—we'll have to look into that this fall."

I picture our red-brick house with some cheerful yellow daffodils. I might not be getting romance out of this marriage, but having a place that's *ours* is nice.

"I like double daffodils better than the regular ones," Jane says.

"Sure." I'm not sure what a double daffodil is, but I don't have strong feelings on types of spring flowers, so I'm happy to do what she wants.

When we arrive at the Canadian Tire nearest to our house, Jane marches inside and leads me through the store. She seems to know what she's doing. I guess she looked up the aisle numbers on her phone while I was driving. She puts a rake and a shovel into our cart, followed by some gloves and pruning shears. At least, I think that's what those are.

And when we get to the lawn mowers, Jane knows exactly what she wants.

"We really need to cut our grass," she says, "so we should buy one today. Is this model okay with you?"

"Um," I say. "It's a lawn mower. I don't know much about them. Whatever you pick is fine with me." Although I cut the grass on occasion when I lived with my parents, I'm far from an expert.

"I couldn't sleep last night, and I did a deep dive into lawn mower reviews."

"Why couldn't you sleep?"

She shrugs. "It happens every now and then, no big deal. Anyway, I thought reading reviews of lawn mowers would be both useful and put me to sleep, but it was surprisingly entertaining. Well, maybe not so much entertaining as interesting. I didn't know there were so many options. What?"

My mouth is hanging open. Somehow, this isn't what I expected from Jane, even though I've known her for a long time.

But admittedly, neither of us had a lawn in all those years.

"You sure you're okay with whatever I like?" she asks.

"Yeah." The one she's picked out isn't the cheapest—and I'm sure there are good reasons for that. "You know more about this than I do."

Once we get home and put all our stuff away, she decides to take the lawn mower out for a spin. She changes into shorts and a tank top, and while she gets to work in the backyard, I start on dinner.

Over the next few days, I learn many things about Jane that I didn't know before.

Reading product reviews is a habit of hers when she can't sleep. She particularly enjoys one-star reviews of both the Bible and laxatives.

I also learn that she likes to exercise first thing in the morning. She buys an elliptical machine for our basement, and we settle into a routine where she gets up and works out, and I have coffee ready for her by the time she's finished her shower.

I give up my Netflix account and learn her password.

"This relationship feels real now," I joke.

I meet our neighbors, too. To our left are the Rosenbaums: a man and woman in their late thirties and their little girl. To the right is a widowed man in his seventies who came over from Hong Kong a few years before my parents.

At the end of every workday, I go for a walk, and I soon find a route I like that takes me about half an hour.

The Friday after our wedding, I return home to find Jane having a snack in the kitchen.

"Are you okay?" She peers at me.

"Yeah, why wouldn't I be?"

"You're sweating a lot. I know it's warm, but it's still fairly pleasant for July."

I hesitate. "A side effect of my antidepressant, which is one of the reasons I hope to go off it eventually. But it's the only drug that worked, so I'm on it for now."

The other irritating side effect of this antidepressant? It killed my libido. Not that it was particularly high when I was severely depressed, but the drug made it worse, even as it improved my mood, and my low sex drive caused problems in my last relationship.

However, there's no reason Jane needs to know about that.

She nods and pours me a glass of water. "That's annoying, but I'm glad you found something. I remember how long it took."

Somehow, we smoothly move to discussing which K-drama we should watch in the evenings, and when we start the first episode after dinner, I pull her against me and she rests her head on my shoulder.

I really do appreciate having someone here, someone who will be a little affectionate with me, someone who will discuss mundane things like weather and lawncare and exercise equipment, even if we aren't sharing a bed.

Even if the last time I kissed her on the lips, it was entirely performative.

Chapter 7

Jane

As I empty the dishwasher, familiar laughter floats through the open kitchen window. I can only hear bits and pieces of the conversation, but it sounds like Evan and the man next door are talking about travel plans. Well, his travel plans—we don't have any.

I figure I should actually meet the neighbor, rather than just waving at him from a distance, so I slide on the flip-flops that I keep by the back door. I walk toward the low fence on the left side of our backyard and put my arm around Evan.

"Hey," I say. The other man is shorter than Evan and has dark curly hair.

"Gordon, this is my wife, Jane," Evan says.

I'm not used to being someone's wife, and it feels strange. Not bad, just...strange. Instinctively, I twist the platinum band on my finger. I haven't fully adjusted to wearing it.

We talk for a few minutes, until someone shouts "Daddy!" from inside the other house, and Gordon says he better get going. I admire Evan's skill at socializing with people he only just met or hasn't known for long. I feel like it takes me a while to get used to someone, but he's already adapted to our new neighborhood.

·❤·❤·❤·❤·❤·

The next morning, I come downstairs after my shower to find my freshly poured coffee on the kitchen table, as always. I appreciate the little routines we've developed.

But today, Evan does something I don't expect.

"Let's go outside," he says.

I give him a puzzled look but follow him to the small back patio. To my surprise, there's actually a place to sit: two black chairs have been pushed under a table.

"I thought we weren't going to spend more money?" I blurt out, gripping my coffee mug. We've bought so much stuff for our house lately, and this looks like a good quality set. Sure, we have money in our joint account—all the gifts from our wedding—but still. "You should have asked..." I trail off, feeling guilty for my outburst. Evan got something nice for me. I just thought we were going to discuss all of our large purchases. That's what we agreed on.

I know finances are one of the biggest sources of conflict in marriage. One of the reasons I agreed to marry him? I thought we were on the same page when it came to such things.

"If it wasn't for the money," he says, "would you be unhappy with it?"

I shake my head.

"I got it for free," he tells me. "I joined a neighborhood group on Facebook. People post stuff they're giving away, and all I had to do was pick it up."

"Someone was giving away their patio furniture? It's in really good condition."

"Isn't it? I'm lucky I saw it as soon as it was posted."

I take a deep breath and exhale slowly. Then I sit down on one of the chairs, and Evan sits down on the other.

"I should have told you that I was getting it," he says.

"No, no," I rush to assure him. "I shouldn't have assumed."

"I promise I won't surprise you with things that cost more than two hundred dollars." He reaches across the small table and clasps one of my hands. His earnestness causes something to clench in my chest.

I shift my chair so it's next to his. It's not like we have an incredible view—just our little backyard with its empty vegetable garden—but it's still pleasant to sit outside on a summer morning. It's supposed to get hot later, but right now, it's not too bad. I sip my coffee and smile.

"In 2020," he says, "it certainly would have been nicer to be here with you, making masks out of old T-shirts and struggling to find toilet paper."

"I agree."

The next day, I leave my home office after I finish work and find Evan in the kitchen.

"I got you another surprise," he says.

"Oh?" I'm about to tell him to wait until I have a snack, but he looks rather excited.

For his job, Evan always wears dress pants and a dress shirt, even if he's just in the basement. He has more meetings than I do, so it makes sense. He used to be a staff accountant, but now he's a financial analyst at a logistics company, and I think the switch has been good for him.

After work, he changes: he's currently wearing shorts and a T-shirt. He's a little sweaty, and there's a dark smudge on the bottom of his shirt. I wonder if that's a clue about my surprise.

He pulls me toward the living room and points out the back door. There's a large outdoor planter, which I assume he got secondhand. Unlike the patio furniture, it doesn't look almost new. Inside the planter is a selection of herbs, and I head outside so I can look at it more closely. Basil, chives, and rosemary.

I remember telling him, the day after our wedding, that I want herbs and cherry tomatoes in our garden, and I know that's why he did it.

I'm not used to seeing evidence that someone is thinking of me. After all, when it comes to my father, I've spent too much time just hoping that he hasn't forgotten my existence. He finally sent me a text to congratulate me on my wedding...a full week after it happened. I'm an afterthought to him.

"Thank you." To my embarrassment, there's a tiny crack in my voice.

They're just herbs. No need to get emotional.

But more than two seconds of thought went into this, and it really is a novelty.

"I'll make you something with them tomorrow," I say. "It'll be hot, so maybe pasta salad with some basil and chives?"

"Sounds good." Evan pauses. "This weekend, there's a retirement dinner for my parents."

"Oh, right," I say. "I forgot about that."

"If you don't want to come, I can make an excuse—"

"No, I want to go. Where is it?"

Years ago, Evan told me that his father loves the Keg, and that's where their small family retirement dinner is held. It's the first time I've seen Evan's family since the wedding, and that makes me nervous for some reason. I've put on a summer dress and actually done my makeup.

"How's married life?" Kim asks. She's sitting across from me, and Evan is to my left.

There are nine of us at a long table on the patio. It's a little too big to have a single conversation; I can only hear bits and pieces of what Howie and Lynne are saying.

"It's good." I reach for a piece of bread and slather it with butter.

"You're not discovering that Evan has all sorts of strange, annoying habits you never knew about before?"

He does have the weird tendency to not stay in the washroom when he brushes his teeth—at least, I find it weird to catch glimpses of him pacing his bedroom and occasionally the upstairs hall—but this is a minor issue.

I shake my head. "Not at all."

"You had to think about it for a moment." She laughs. "I admit it was a bit of an adjustment when Max and I moved in together. Not that I wasn't ready—he had a detailed list of things we had to figure out before living together, and we followed it—but still. I was so used to living alone."

"Me, too. But I think it's less adjustment, in some ways, because we have lots of space." Max and Kim live in a two-bedroom apartment in a newish building, not far from downtown. Downtown Toronto, that is, not downtown Richmond Hill. "Owning a place is definitely an adjustment, though."

The other day, the handle on the downstairs toilet broke off, and my first thought was that we should call the landlord. Then I remembered that there is no landlord.

No, it's just us.

Really, it wasn't so bad. I went to the store, got the part, and repaired it myself after watching a YouTube video. It gave me a sense of accomplishment, and I didn't have to bug anyone to fix it.

Living with Evan is more of an adjustment than I let on, to be honest—but in a good way. He really has been very attentive.

I fear if I talk about it, though, it'll sound like we didn't have a proper relationship beforehand, and he told me that he believes his family has gotten over their initial suspicions.

"What are you going to do with all your time now?" Yvonne asks Howie and Lynne, and Kim and I turn our attention to the other end of the table.

"Maybe one of you will give us grandchildren," Howie says with a laugh.

Though I'm not opposed to the idea of children, my hand freezes in front of my mouth, tasty bread forgotten. Given that Evan and I are the ones who are married, I feel like this comment might be directed at us.

"Dad..." Evan says.

Lynne leans toward her husband and whispers something in his ear.

"Ah, why not?" Howie says. "I'm not pressuring them. Just saying. I have free time to help with babies now."

"I'm not having children," Leo grunts.

"Okay. You can learn how to play golf with me. I always wanted to try."

Leo opens his mouth—presumably to reject that idea—but before he can speak, the server arrives with our steaks.

"Jane, can I talk to you?" Lynne asks after we exit the restaurant.

Before I can answer, she leads me a few steps away from everyone else, and my heart rate kicks up. I feel like I'm about to get in trouble.

"Howie and I think you should go on a honeymoon."

I must look a little shocked, because she says, "Don't worry, this has nothing to do with us wanting grandchildren."

I hadn't made that connection in my mind. I probably look even more shocked now.

"I know you're being careful with your money," she continues, "but you didn't have a fancy wedding, either. You deserve a little trip this summer, yes? We will pay—"

"No," I say. "You don't need—"

"A *little* trip," she emphasizes. "We're not paying for you to go to Paris. Well, maybe Paris, Ontario. I'm not sure what's there. We just thought you could have a nice weekend away. A few nights in a bed and breakfast? I have some picked out..." She takes out her phone.

I wonder if she's had so much time to do this because she's retired, even if it's only been a week.

"You should ask Evan," I say.

He ought to take the lead when it comes to his parents, right? Besides, I don't have much experience with trying to refuse things from older relatives, and I want his parents to like me. I fear that if this conversation goes on much longer, I will have agreed to numerous things that I certainly don't need.

"Aiyah!" Lynne says. "I already did. He said no."

Oh my God. Does she think I'm the weakest link? Is she two seconds away from stuffing an envelope of cash into my hand? I'm fine with accepting fruit and leftovers—I truly appreciate the thought—but this is different. I don't want to feel like I'm in debt to them.

To my relief, Evan appears at my side and puts his arm around me. "Mom! As I told you, you don't need to pay for a honeymoon. Please tell me you didn't make a nonrefundable reservation."

She clucks her tongue. "I'm not *that* interfering. But you should go on a trip."

"Why are you so set on this?"

Lynne huffs and mutters something in Cantonese, but I don't speak the language.

Then Howie joins us. "You need to put effort into your marriage from the very beginning. Don't forget about the romance."

I'm moderately horrified. Why are they actually saying this out loud?

Now it feels like everyone has gathered around. Jon is laughing. Max is frowning at Evan, for reasons I don't understand.

"Mom," Evan says in a firm tone that I've never heard from him before, though he still has a smile on his face, "really, we're fine. You and Dad should go somewhere with the money instead. You have lots of time and, as you've reminded us, no grandchildren."

Lynne seems to accept this...for now.

We say our goodbyes and head to the car. On the drive home, I ask Evan if he's worried that his parents have become suspicious about our relationship again.

"I don't think so," he says.

"What about Max?"

"No, he's just a little miffed that I kept you a secret for so long. Not from our parents, but from him."

"Oh. I don't know anything about having siblings. I mean, I do have siblings, but they're a lot younger than me. It's not quite the same." I pause. "I hope you don't want to speed up the whole discussion-about-having-children thing because of what your parents said?"

"No. I'm not ready yet. We'll talk about it next summer."

·❤·❤·❤·❤·❤·

As I get ready for bed, I'm overtaken by an urge that I haven't had since before I was a married woman. In horror, I wonder if it's because of the talk of us having children, but no. I think it's just random.

Or is it related to the thought of going on a honeymoon with...someone?

I take my only vibrator out of its hiding spot, turn it on, and push aside my underwear. When I masturbate, I don't think of sex, not exactly. Rather, it's the feeling of being in bed with a man I want to have sex with. The *feeling* of being in love like that.

Something along those lines. I don't even know how to describe it. Just whatever I can do to get myself off as fast as possible and rid myself of this inconvenient need.

Occasionally, I wish sex was something I wanted separately from love. Many years ago, I had a female friend who said that if guys could have casual sex without shame, then we should, too. When I told her it wasn't something I wanted, even if it weren't for the possible slut-shaming and danger of violence, she said I was a bad feminist and should free myself of my patriarchal mindset. I tried to convince her that this wasn't the "problem," such as it was, and she assumed I was a lesbian.

It was a while before I figured out that I'm on the ace spectrum, something I initially assumed I couldn't be because I do have sexual urges.

Anyway, I'm fine with the way my body works now. I really am. But I think it's human nature to occasionally wish that our lives could be a little different from what they actually are.

And that I did, for example, want to spend a whole weekend in a hotel room with my new husband.

Chapter 8

Evan

I can't believe my mother ambushed Jane after the retirement dinner. Mom isn't usually so pushy. I'll have to keep a closer eye on her so she doesn't scare off my poor wife. I really want them to have a good relationship, especially given the absence of other maternal figures in Jane's life.

And somehow, this is all related to why I'm now hauling my giant penguin plushie downstairs while Jane is mowing the front lawn. I want to cheer her up, and this makes sense in my head. Obviously, a chubby penguin named Watson won't make up for my interfering family, but it's what I have on hand.

The plushie was actually a gift from an old boyfriend, but I like it, and it seemed a shame to throw it out just because we broke up, though it lived in the basement at my parents' house for a while. But now, I have a house of my own that has room for stuff like this, and he's been peacefully sitting in my walk-in closet.

Until now.

I set him by the back sliding door. After looking at the white-and-black plushie for a few seconds, I decide he needs more, for lack of a better word, *pizzazz*. I head back to my closet and peruse the options, eventually deciding that Watson would look dashing in a flamboyant purple scarf that I haven't worn in years. Unfortunately, Watson's neck (or lack thereof) is much fatter than mine, and I can't quite get the look I'd hoped to achieve, but by the time I hear Jane turn off the mower—I think she's moving to the backyard now—Watson is ready for her arrival.

Jane always mows from the left to right side of the backyard, and the back door is to the right. Watson and I watch her go back and forth a few times, and then, as she's pushing the mower toward the house, she looks in our direction. Watson waves as best he can with his flipper.

She tilts her head curiously...and then a smile graces her face. It's beautiful.

She turns off the mower and walks toward us in the old running shoes that she uses for cutting the lawn. As she steps onto the mat—one of our other Canadian Tire purchases—my heart kicks up a notch, which is strange.

I hand her a water bottle. She nods in thanks. Weirdly, I find myself watching her throat as she takes a few gulps.

"What's the penguin doing here?" she asks.

He thought you needed a laugh after your in-laws tried to force you to go on vacation.

Since that sounds a little too ridiculous to say out loud, I go for, "He wanted to see you cut the grass." I speak in a *this-is-only-sensible* voice.

Her lips curve up again, and I'm unreasonably pleased to have caused this reaction.

"Where did you get him?" she asks.

"I've had him for a while. He was a gift from...an ex." For some reason, I feel weird about admitting that, even though she knows I have many exes. She even met most of them.

"What's his name?"

"Watson," I reply. "I found it on a list of suggested names for penguins. I thought it suited him better than 'Flip' or 'Snowball' or 'Washington,' which were some of the other names on the list."

"Does he have a last name?"

"No. 'Watson' is a mononym."

"Well, I hope he enjoys the show."

She goes outside and turns the mower on. I watch her ass as she moves toward the back of the yard...

Wait a second. Why am I staring at my wife's ass in those little jean shorts?

I give my head a shake and continue to regard her as she turns around and heads back toward the house. She gives me a little smile, and oh God, that isn't helping.

Her parting words ring in my ears.

I hope he enjoys the show.

Maybe the smile was just for Watson, but the truth is that I really like watching Jane cut the grass in her shorts and tank top and old sneakers. And when I try to think of something else, I picture her skin glistening with sweat, her throat working as she swallowed the water.

I flee to my office in the basement, which is thankfully cooler and doesn't afford any views of Jane in the backyard. I plop down on my desk chair.

Why on earth am I feeling a prickle of attraction toward my *wife*?

This wasn't supposed to happen. I've known her for well over a decade, and it's never happened before. Could I appreciate that she's a pretty woman? Sure. But it's never been quite like this, and I *know* she doesn't feel this way about me.

In most cases, being attracted to your spouse is the very opposite of a problem, but this wasn't part of our deal. Sex is something that I'm supposed to get outside of marriage, with one exception: if we decide to try for a baby, once we've been married for a year.

Reminding myself of that isn't improving the situation.

Desperately, I try to think of another topic, and my mind jumps to my family. Okay, that's good. That'll help. But then I remember how my parents encouraged us to go on a honeymoon, which would mean being in a hotel room with Jane...

This really isn't working.

I rest my elbows on the desk and put my head in my hands. It's probably just happening because I haven't had sex in over a year. Also, I haven't taken care of myself in a while.

Yes, that must be the problem. Apparently, neglecting my own needs is causing unwanted attraction to the woman who's living with me. My libido isn't as high as it used to be, but it's not nonexistent.

I go upstairs to my bedroom and make quick work of it, trying to keep my wife out of my mind while I touch myself. Then I clean up and come back downstairs. Jane is inside now—I guess she's finished cutting the grass.

"So," I say, stuffing my hands in my pockets, "what do you want for dinner?"

Tuesday morning, while Jane is in the shower after her workout and I'm waiting for the coffee, I decide that Watson should start the day with a new outfit. I remove his bright scarf and set a cowboy hat on his head. Don't ask why I have one of those, but I do.

Jane's schedule is predictable, and when I expect her downstairs in the next minute or two, I pour our coffee and take it outside, setting both mugs on the patio table. She soon emerges and sits next to me.

"Thanks," she says.

Although it's not even eight o'clock, it's already pretty warm. It's going to be a hot one.

As we have our first coffee, we usually talk about our plans for the day, what we have to do for work. My job is mostly remote, which has its advantages, but I'm one of those people who genuinely liked working in an office. Not at my first job out of school—the guy in the next cubicle was a loud asshole who constantly interrupted me—but in general, I enjoyed it.

Today, however, Jane is quiet. She stares at a bird sitting on the fence.

"It's my mom's birthday," she says at last. "She would have been sixty."

I reach over and squeeze her hand; she doesn't look at me.

"I've been thinking about her more lately. I always do, when big life events happen—like getting married and buying a house." Her gaze flits over to me. Then she looks forward again, toward the bird, but I don't think she's really paying attention to her surroundings.

I don't say anything. I think she just needs someone to listen.

She's talked about her mom with me before, but not a lot. I had the impression of a playful, involved mother, though Jane was quick to point out that her childhood memories may not, exactly, be the truth. I also know that her mom died of cervical cancer.

In the silence, I do some quick math. I know how old Jane was when she lost her mom...

"She was thirty-two," I say as realization dawns. "Is that why you wanted to wait until you were thirty-three to get engaged?"

She nods. "I knew it was unlikely that I wouldn't live to see my thirty-third birthday, but some tiny part of me couldn't quite believe that I'd make it."

I open my mouth to say I'm sorry, but for some reason, I don't think she wants to hear it. I keep my hand on hers and squeeze it again. It seems wrong that someone could die of cancer at such a young age, but her mom is hardly the only one.

"I wish I could have met her," I say simply.

"I wish so, too."

If only I could take that pain from her face, but I can't. Her mother died a long time ago, and nothing can bring her back.

"Do you want to do anything for her birthday?" I ask.

Jane is quiet for a moment. "We should have cake."

"Okay. What did she like—what would you like?" I can't bake, and I'm not familiar with the bakeries in the area, but I see it as my job, as her husband, to procure something.

"We can just have some of our wedding cake. I mean, we should use it up, right?"

"Yes, but if you want something else—"

"No, the wedding cake is good. Slices of vanilla, not chocolate. My mom always picked vanilla, if given the choice, and I never understood."

Since I'm determined to do my very best when it comes to this simple task, I google it on my phone. Apparently, it's best to defrost cake by putting it in the fridge the day before. It's cut up into slices, however, so I figure twelve hours shouldn't be a problem.

We sit there, sipping our coffee, for a few more minutes, my hand loosely holding hers. Even in that short period of time, I swear I can feel the outside temperature rising. I'll be glad to be in my basement office for the workday, but for now, I'm here with Jane.

When she stands up, I feel more disappointed than I should. But a split second later, her quiet laughter fills the air, and it brings me more joy than expected.

I turn around. Jane is looking at Watson, who has yet to remove his cowboy hat.

"Yee-haw," she says, her tone a little dry.

I can't contain my grin.

I go for a longer walk than usual at the end of the workday, and I buy a package of candles and some matches. After dinner, I put one slice of defrosted vanilla wedding cake on a plate for Jane, and the other on a plate for me. I slide a candle into her slice.

"Make a wish," I say after lighting the candle.

Maybe she'll wish for something impossible; maybe she'll wish for something small.

I just want her to be able to dream.

Chapter 9

Jane

"How's marriage and home ownership?" Claudia asks me the next day on a video call.

I'm sitting on my bed after dinner. Evan is outside, talking to Gordon, and later, we'll watch an episode of our current K-drama. Evan told me yesterday that he thinks the lead actor is hot, and I felt a strange prickle of jealousy.

"It's good," I say.

It seems like such an insufficient word. *Good.*

"It's just what I wanted," I add. "I have a proper home office and a yard to care for. Someone to eat meals and watch TV with me. It might not be exciting, but it's nice."

Claudia gives me a strange look.

"What?" I say.

"I'm not an expert in this sort of thing," she begins, "but I was thinking of your marriage as a queerplatonic relationship, and now, I'm not so sure. Something about your expression..."

"I don't know what you're talking about," I say automatically. "I'm not falling in love—romantic love—with my husband, which is what you seem to be getting at. Just because we cuddle and hold hands sometimes—"

"This is *me* you're talking to. I get it."

I sigh. "Even when I do fall in love, I don't look starry-eyed."

"Are you sure?"

I roll my eyes. "It's just pleasant. Comfortable."

Claudia has a couple of friends who are sharing a home and raising their kids together, without being romantically involved. They're what comes to mind when I think of a queerplatonic relationship. But why does it feel weird to use that language for me and Evan? I'm not sure, but I know it's not because I'm falling for him.

"It doesn't feel suffocating?" she asks. "To be around each other so often?"

"No. I..." I trail off as I consider the fact that Evan doesn't go out as much as I thought he might. I mean, he goes for walks and talks to the neighbors, but I was always under the impression that he had many friend groups and a much more active social life than I do.

I haven't seen evidence of that, though.

"It's nice." It's the second time I've used that word, but I'm not sure what else to say. "Like, yesterday was my mom's birthday, and I was glad I wasn't alone all day. I asked him to take out some frozen wedding cake, and he lit a candle and told me to make a wish."

"What did you wish for?"

"For our marriage to continue to be good. That's all."

I never wanted anything big from life. Maybe it's because my mom died when I was so young. I had to deal with that profound loss, and I didn't imagine things like, I don't know, becoming an astronaut.

No, living to thirty-three and owning a house seems like enough. A house where I feel like I belong, even if I've been here for less than a month. By the time I was a teenager, I felt like an outsider in the place where I'd grown up. Suzanne had moved in, and every picture of my mother—aside from those in my room—had been put away. I couldn't be myself there, but I can here.

If some tiny part of me wanted a romance, well, being married to a nice man with a nice family should suffice.

Speaking of that family...

"His parents tried to convince us to go on a honeymoon and offered to pay for it. His mom confronted me since Evan had already said no."

"But he has your back when dealing with his family?"

"Yeah, and they're usually fine. It's just that one incident."

I find myself fiddling with the band on my finger and thinking of the gift he gave me earlier. A tiny ceramic dish, made by a local artist—I assume he got it at the market that he went to the other day—to hold my ring when I'm cooking. My platonic feelings for him are deepening, but I expected that to happen, once we started spending so much time together.

"I'm glad it's going well," Claudia says. "I'm just a little worried that one of you will change what you want from this marriage."

I shake my head. "Enough about me. Now tell me about the drama in your D&D group."

"How long do you have?"

By the time I go downstairs, it's getting dark, and Evan is closing the vertical blinds at our back door. The action knocks down Watson's umbrella. The forecast called for rain, and it did end up raining a little around lunch; I guess that's why Evan went with an umbrella today. After he finishes closing the blinds, he carefully fixes the umbrella, and I look around the room.

"This room needs something else," I say.

"Like what?" he asks.

"Maybe a plant or two? But I don't know anything about houseplants."

"You should ask Yvonne. I'll give you her number, and you can text her."

"Oh. Um. Are you sure she'd be okay with that?"

"Why not?"

I guess I didn't imagine having relationships with anyone in Evan's family separate from him—and does he think of Yvonne, who's been dating Leo for under a year, as family?

He comes over to me and sets his hands on my shoulder. "I'm happy to ask her instead, if it makes you uncomfortable."

"No, no, I'll text her."

A few minutes later, I send Yvonne a message. I snap a picture of the room and tell her that it faces north-ish—I don't know if that's important, but it might be.

She immediately starts sending me links to pretty plants, and I can't help but smile.

Our first houseplant arrives, unexpectedly, on Saturday evening.

At Lana's insistence, Evan and I agreed to hold a small housewarming party. At five o'clock, he drives to Finch Station to pick up our friends, while I stay back and finish preparing the food. I'm not usually much of a hostess, but then again, I've never had a house before. Evan suggested we buy frozen appetizers that simply needed to be baked in the oven, but I wanted to make my own. And so here I am, preparing brie bites and spinach feta bites.

With purchased puff pastry, of course—I'm not that much of a masochist.

Still, in my flowered apron, I feel like a housewife, even if the apron is my husband's. Personally, I'd have bought something less bright and colorful.

At the sound of a key in the front door, I throw the muffin tin with the brie bites into the oven, set the timer, and head out to greet our guests, feeling more nervous than I usually would at the idea of seeing longtime friends.

"Jane!" Ash hugs me with one arm. "I can't believe you own a *house* now. Red bricks, a garage, and everything. Here, I got you a bunny ear cactus. I wasn't sure what to buy for a housewarming gift because I don't know anyone else who actually owns a house."

I take the cactus from his hands. "Thanks for coming."

"Nice apron. It's Evan's, isn't it?"

Evan laughs from the back of the group. "Of course it is."

Ash is one of those people who's more a member of my friend group than an actual friend. I find him a bit much in large quantities but am happy to see him at group events. He and Evan dated briefly, though it was a long time ago now.

Lana and Camila enter the house after Ash. Camila is carrying the charcuterie tray that she promised to bring.

"It's a shark-cuterie board," she says, "but you'll have to eat some of the prosciutto before you can see the shark."

"I won't have any trouble doing that," Evan says.

"The board itself is your housewarming gift, by the way."

Behind Lana and Camila is Georgie, who doesn't say much but pulls a bottle of white wine out of their hoodie.

Everyone takes off their shoes in the front hall, and I meet Evan's eyes. "How was the drive?"

"Not too bad," he says. "A stalled bus caused a back-up near the station, but otherwise, about as good as you could expect."

We give our guests a quick tour, beginning with the kitchen. In the living room, Watson—decked out in a rainbow lei—is the main attraction. Next, we head to the dining room, which is mostly empty, unfortunately. We still need to buy furniture for it, but it hasn't been a huge priority. Ash is impressed by our "in-unit laundry," and Lana appreciates the fact that we have multiple washrooms.

But as we climb the stairs, I feel a bit anxious. When we arranged this little party, I wasn't thinking about everyone seeing our bedrooms.

"This is my room," I say, opening the door a crack. "Looks like the bedroom in my old apartment, basically."

"You have separate bedrooms?" Ash says. "That's smart. I wish we could do that. Jer sends his regrets, by the way, but he couldn't get out of work."

"The extra closet space would certainly be nice." Lana sighs.

I swear Georgie gives me an odd look because of the bedroom situation. However, I'm saved when the oven timer goes off and I have to head downstairs, leaving Evan to finish the tour.

We gather in the living room, the food on the coffee table. There isn't a ton of seating, so I sit on the floor in front of Evan and reach for a brie bite. It's very good, if I do say so myself, though it's hard to screw up something that's centered around warm cheese. The wine is good, too. It's the first time I've had a drink since the wedding.

"I still can't get over the fact that you two are *together*," Ash says.

I stiffen a little, but I don't think anyone notices. Except Evan, who rubs my shoulder.

"You were at our wedding," he points out to Ash.

"I *know*. Speaking of which, do you have your pictures yet?"

"No," I say, "but I think we're supposed to get them next week."

"I can't wait to see them."

I focus on the charcuterie plate, trying to decide which cheese looks best.

"I'm curious about chores," Lana says.

"Chores?" Ash rolls his eyes and takes a glug of wine. "Why are you curious about that?"

"Who does what?"

"Jane does the yardwork and the majority of the cooking," Evan says. "I do the laundry and most of the cleaning."

At least, I think that's what he says, but he's continuing the rub my shoulders, and he hits the perfect point that nearly makes me moan. Is he doing this to convince everyone that we're a real couple?

I don't like the idea, for some reason. I hope he's doing it because he wants to, and I try not to think about my recent conversation with Claudia.

Our friends insist on taking an Uber to the subway rather than depending on Evan for another ride. (He rarely drinks and didn't have any alcohol tonight, so he'd be perfectly capable of driving.) They hug us and stumble out into the night, in various states of inebriation, and we finish cleaning up. I pop the final piece of prosciutto into my mouth, followed by a grape, before I put the remaining food in a large glass container. Evan, meanwhile, loads up the dishwasher.

We work in silence for a couple of minutes before he says, "I think that went well."

"Me, too."

"It's nice to have a big enough place to properly entertain. I always wanted that."

I'm about to put the container in the fridge when I realize there's a single cube of the best cheese left. I have no idea what kind of cheese it is, but it's really good and lightly smoky. Before I know what I'm doing, I walk over to Evan, who's cleaning the muffin tin. His hands are in soapy water, so I can't actually hand him the cheese. Oh well. I stand on my toes and hold it to his lips. I'm just being practical, right? He hesitates for a split second before pulling the piece of cheese into his mouth, his lower lip brushing my fingers.

"Mm. That's delicious," he says. "I didn't have any earlier. I guess I was too busy inhaling your brie bites." He knocks his hip against mine.

Perhaps it's the wine—I had two generous glasses—but I feel an unusual amount of pleasure at his compliment. At the smile aimed in my direction.

A little flustered, I take out the broom and give the kitchen floor a good sweep.

Chapter 10

Evan

The Monday after our wine and cheese gathering, I set our morning coffee on the kitchen table. It's raining, unfortunately, so we can't sit outside.

When Jane comes downstairs, she says, "Did you check your email? We got the link to the gallery for our wedding pictures."

I sit next to her and take a sip from my mug—the one with the rainbow umbrella seemed appropriate today—before picking up my phone. I navigate to the gallery and enter the password that was provided.

The photos are in chronological order. We didn't have the photographer take pictures of us getting ready, but there are a few pre-ceremony pictures of everyone mingling outside. One of my father with his hand on my shoulder; another of Jane talking to Auntie Gladys. (Well, I suspect my aunt was doing most of the talking.)

My gaze is drawn to the photos of Jane. I feel like I didn't properly admire her on our wedding day, and I'm annoyed with myself. I mean, I told her that she looked great, but I don't remember her looking like *this*. She has a soft glow about her that's captivating.

I get to the picture of us kissing at the end of the ceremony. It looks slightly awkward—or maybe I'm just remembering how it felt in the moment.

I wish I could redo it.

I glance up at the woman next to me. She's wearing a simple black T-shirt, and her brow is furrowed in concentration as she stares at her phone.

"We'll have to pick something for our thank-you cards," she says. "Not that we need to decide now, but we should get those sorted in the next couple of months."

"Yeah."

She sets down her phone and turns to me. It's quiet in our house; all I can hear is the rain pattering on the patio.

"Do you not like the pictures?" she asks.

Oh God. Is it my expression? The tone of my voice when I gave that one-word answer?

Evan, you're an idiot.

"No, no," I rush to assure her. "I love them. She did a great job. I'm just not fully awake yet."

I continue studying the photos. After the ceremony and receiving line, the photographer took pictures of us with my family, then spent about ten minutes taking pictures of just the two of us. When we were discussing what we wanted, before the wedding, she suggested a few other locations nearby where we could have romantic shots, but we declined.

And now, I kick myself for that.

I zoom in on one of the pictures. We're standing in the small garden at the venue, and Jane is looking up at me with a fond smile. Was she faking that? Or is it real?

"We should get a large print to hang on the wall," I say. "Maybe this one?" I show her the picture that's captured my attention, but I'm not sure I actually want to see it every day.

I might obsess over it.

· ❤ · ❤ · ❤ · ❤ · ❤ ·

By the middle of Monday morning, it's clear it's going to be a rather hellish week for me at work. Last-minute meetings eat up time that I desperately need. Though I don't tell Jane much about it, I think she notices.

When I get up on Wednesday, I head downstairs and find Watson sitting on a kitchen chair. I release a surprised laugh. He isn't wearing any accessories, but there's a mug in front of him that simply says, in large letters, "Fuck." (One of Jane's mugs, not mine.)

This is the first time she's moved Watson. She's not around to see my reaction; no, she must be on the elliptical machine in the basement.

When we're sitting outside with our coffee—I've stolen the "fuck" mug; I hope Watson doesn't mind—Jane makes no mention of the earlier scene in the kitchen.

Instead, she says, "We've spent a lot of time at home lately."

"We have. I thought that's what you like?"

"I do, but how about we go out for dinner this Friday?"

I shouldn't be so excited that my wife is asking me on a date, of sorts, but I am. "Where should we go?"

"Leave that to me," she says.

"Evan, are you ready?"

"Just a minute!" I call, but there's no way I'll be able to fix this mess in a minute. I sigh and take out the makeup remover.

A moment later, there's a knock on the half-open door of my en suite, and Jane pokes her head in. She's wearing some kind of gauzy black shirt, and her lips are red. She looks at what's strewn across the counter.

"Were you trying to put on eyeshadow?" she asks.

"'Trying' is the key word, yes," I say.

Aside from the wedding, I haven't worn makeup in a while, but I felt the urge to do so today. I'm not entirely sure why. Maybe because my life has seemed so conservative lately? Marriage, house in the suburbs. Or it has something to do with the rough week I've survived.

I sigh. "It's fine, we can go."

Jane steps into the bathroom. Her outfit has a striking silhouette. She's wearing wide-legged pinstripe black pants and an asymmetrical top that exposes her left shoulder, but not her right. She's always favored black clothes when dressing up.

I know I've seen her wear that shirt before, but it's somehow different today. I want to slide the other sleeve down and bare her right shoulder. I want...

I should not be lusting after my wife.

I move toward the door of the washroom, but she doesn't step back to allow me to pass. She's mere inches from me now, and that's not helping.

"I can do it for you," she says.

"No, it's okay. We don't have time." I don't know where we're going; she just told me when to be ready.

She looks at her watch. "It's fine. I checked the traffic, and it's not too bad. If we leave in twenty minutes, we'll be a couple of minutes late, at most."

I hesitate. "Okay." Then I pull out my phone and show her a short video. "This is what I was trying to do."

The person in the video is white and doesn't have mono-lids like I do. Combined with the fact that I haven't done this a while, I wasn't happy with my efforts.

Jane nods, then lifts herself onto the counter so she's taller than I am.

"Are you sure you're okay with this?" I ask as she opens up the flame eyeshadow palette.

"Yeah. I know you rarely see me wear eyeshadow"—it looks like she's wearing eyeliner and mascara right now, nothing more—"but I'm pretty good at it. I didn't have a mother or older sister to teach me about makeup, so at some point, I made a dedicated effort to teach myself." She picks up a brush.

"That wasn't what I, uh, meant," I say as she starts working on my face. I've worn bold makeup in public with Jane before, but I'm very aware of the fact that we now have matching wedding bands. "One of the women I dated—not for long—she didn't like when I did anything that would mark me as...not necessarily straight."

Jane frowns. "Then why was she dating a queer guy? I assume she knew."

"Yeah." I'd told her that I was bi, though now I usually call myself queer because it feels more comfortable. "I think she liked being able to discuss men—you know, movie stars and stuff—with me. She liked when it felt theoretical? But when, for example, she learned that I'd actually slept with men, it made her uneasy."

Jane pauses in her work. "Well, that's fucking bullshit."

I manage a chuckle. "I know."

"Nothing—about this, I mean—has changed now that we're married."

"I didn't really think—" I begin.

"No, it's fine. I get it." She's looking very intently at my eyes. Her tongue peaks out from between her red lips. I'm captivated by her closeness, by the sight of her focusing on something.

On me.

Having her do my makeup...it feels very intimate.

She tips up my chin with a single finger, and I yearn to feel her entire hand trailing down my neck.

Get it together, Evan.

Finally, she gives me a brisk nod. "Not bad. Tell me what you think." She hops down from the counter. "I think you look hot."

I can't focus on my reflection because that word is echoing in my head.

Hot.

I know she doesn't mean it in an *I-want-to-get-you-naked* way, but still.

"Is it okay?" she asks.

Oh no. Now I've been quiet for too long and she's worried I don't like it.

I squeeze her hand. "Yeah, I love it."

Jane drives us east along 16th. She parks in a lot in Unionville and leads me to a Greek restaurant in a converted house. The hostess takes us to a table under a red umbrella on the front patio. Baskets of flowers hang on the white fence.

"This is lovely," I say. "Have you been here before?"

Jane shakes her head. "No, I was just looking for something with a nice patio."

She busies herself with the menu, while I spend another few seconds looking around. It's the sort of place that could be on a listicle of romantic patios in the Greater Toronto Area, but I remind myself that she doesn't mean it to be *romantic*.

We debate getting the platter for two, then decide it's too much food—it would probably be enough to serve at least three. I opt for the lamb shank, and she chooses the quail. For appetizers, we eventually settle on melitzanosalata, which I've never had before, but it sounds a bit like baba ganouj. Jane also wants to get the taramasalata.

"Would you like a drink?" I ask. "I'm happy to drive home."

Once she selects a white wine and we place our order, there's a moment of awkward silence. I feel slightly off-kilter.

"Any plans for the weekend?" she asks.

"I have a bunch of laundry to do tomorrow, and Watson thought he'd like a plant friend, one that isn't a prickly cactus. We could go to Home Depot?"

I know, I know, it's an incredibly mundane conversation for a first date, but I don't mind.

It's strange that I'm thinking of this as a first date, though. Jane and I hung out many times, just the two of us, while engaged—although, to be fair, we were mostly trying to figure out logistical stuff and rarely went out to eat.

It's not a date. It's a meal with a friend.

Jane's wine arrives. She murmurs her thanks, then tries a sip. Her lipstick leaves a faint smudge on the glass, and I shouldn't find that mesmerizing, but I do.

Fortunately, before I can fixate on it too much, the server brings over our dips. I swipe some of the pale-pink taramasalata up with my pita. The color is from the roe, and I think the base is crustless white bread.

Jane doesn't say much as she helps herself to the dips. I try not to stare on her lips and her throat as she eats, but then I drop my gaze to her single bare shoulder—and for some reason, that doesn't help.

"Do you like it?" She gestures at the food. "I feel like I'm eating twice as fast as you."

"I do, I do." I pick up my pace and try to stop admiring her. I don't succeed.

But the dips are delicious, and our mains are equally tasty. I give Jane some of my lamb, and she murmurs her approval.

It really is a nice night, and I'm done with work for the week. An older white woman gives me an odd look as she walks by—the eye makeup, presumably—but I brush it off pretty easily. I tell myself it was just my imagination, even though it probably wasn't.

After dinner, we walk up and down Main Street before returning to the car.

"You know," Jane says as I pull out of the parking lot, "I think Home Depot is still open. Should we go now?"

"Sure, why not? You'll have to give me directions, though."

She directs me to the most convenient location, and as we step out of the car, I'm conscious of the fact that we're not dressed for buying plants at Home Depot. Jane is wearing a sophisticated black outfit with stilettos, for God's sake. But if she wants to do it now while we're out, I'm game. I put on my mask, and we head into the store.

"We should get something big for the living room," I suggest. "To sit on the floor and cover Watson's head. Maybe one of these?" I point to some kind of palm.

"I like this one better." Jane gestures to at a mass cane plant—I know what it is only because I can read.

"Fine with me. What about a Boston fern?"

"Put it in the cart."

"Ooh, look!" I say. "This one is called a Swiss cheese vine. Don't you like cheese?"

She considers the hole-y plant for a moment and nods. "Sure, why not?"

By the time we leave the store—five minutes before clos-ing—we've spent over a hundred dollars on plants and a variety of other things, and I laugh as I jog with the cart toward the car, Jane jogging beside me despite her heels.

She starts to load our purchases into the car. "Shit."

"What is it?" I ask.

"The mass—whatever. The tall plant. How are we going to get it home?"

I look at my hatchback, then the plant, and start laughing. "Maybe we should return it?"

She twists her lips. "No, we'll try to make it work. We'll put everything else in first, and I'll sit in the backseat to babysit it."

In the end, we push forward the passenger's seat, set the mass cane on the floor behind it, and tip the plant to the side. Jane sits behind the driver's seat and holds on to the plant's trunk. She moves a leaf out of the way so she can close the door.

"Ready?" I ask, fastening my seatbelt.

"Let's go," she says.

We manage to get the plants into our house with only a small amount of spilled dirt, which I promptly clean up.

"Where should we put them?" I ask.

"We'll need to look up what conditions they prefer. Or ask Yvonne. We can do that tomorrow. For now..." Jane sets the largest plant near the back door and carefully places Watson underneath.

For some reason, seeing Jane in her going-out clothes, gently positioning a large plushie, causes a rush of amused fondness in my chest. If I'm honest with myself, the intensity is unlike what I would have felt if I'd seen her doing such a thing even a few weeks ago.

I'm not sure I want to be honest.

"What do you want to do now?" she asks. "I need to get out of these clothes…"

She says something after that, but I'm not paying attention. I'm thinking of her sitting on the bathroom counter as she did my makeup. I'm thinking of removing that shirt with the same care she showed Watson. Brushing her nipple—

"Evan?" she says.

"I was just thinking…we didn't take any pictures of us. That seems like a mistake. Since we both look nice. Even if you have dirt on your pants now."

She looks down and wipes it off, and I try to get myself under control.

"You're right," she says at last. "You look really good tonight. You deserve a picture."

I hand her my phone before sitting beside Watson and the plant on the carpet, which earns me a chuckle that I find more delightful than I should. Especially after her compliment—though I tell myself she was just complimenting her own work.

She takes a couple of pictures, and then I beckon her onto the couch. When she sits down, I join her, and I hold my phone up for a selfie.

"Is this really necessary?" she mutters, but she leans closer to me for the picture.

I take a few before telling her that I need a shower. "Want to watch an episode afterward?" I don't say which show, but she'll know.

"Sure."

Upstairs, I inspect my face in the mirror before removing the makeup, then pop a gummy. I take a cool shower, which I hope will be enough to douse the physical attraction I feel toward Jane, since this was very much not part of the deal.

When I return to the living room, she's dressed in shorts and a T-shirt, and she has our next episode ready to go.

"I had a gummy," I tell her. "You want one?"

"No, I think the wine was enough."

She curls up against me, and I start the third episode of a contemporary K-drama. Throughout the entire episode, I'm conscious of her closeness, but at least my earlier lust has faded. Somewhat.

Just before eleven, I pat Watson on the head before Jane and I go upstairs together. Outside her bedroom door, I give her a lingering hug.

"Thanks for tonight," I say.

As she heads into her room without me, it feels so wrong. I want to go with her. I want to fall asleep next to her and wake up next to her. We're a little affectionate with each other, and we cuddle while we watch TV and movies, but somehow, that's not enough.

I want to touch her even more.

But I don't tell her any of that, just retreat to my bedroom.

Chapter 11

Jane

I DON'T WORK OUT on the weekends. I let myself to sleep in, although lately, I've only been able to sleep until eight. When I was younger, I could sleep until at least ten if I didn't set an alarm, but those days have passed.

I get dressed and pad downstairs. I'm the first one up today—often the case on Saturdays—so I make the morning coffee. When it's ready, I pour mine into one of Evan's mugs. It says "caffeine" and "chaos" on it, and the latter is not a word I'd ever use to describe myself, but I delight in the inappropriateness of it.

I've been sitting outside, enjoying the quiet grayness of the day, for ten minutes when Evan emerges. He takes a seat beside me. Neither of us immediately speaks, but that doesn't seem weird. We see each other all the time; sometimes we have no words to say.

His phone buzzes, and he takes a look. "My parents are going to a restaurant near us for lunch. They'll stop by afterward with some food, if that's okay?"

"Sure," I say.

"I'm planning on running some errands and visiting Isobel later. You're welcome to come, but you don't need to."

"I'll stay home."

I like the idea of having some space, truth be told. I wouldn't say I'm getting sick of Evan, but I lived alone for so long, and I crave some time by myself.

He squeezes my hand before sipping his coffee.

Much of our morning is spent on chores, but that's okay. It's nice to have a place that's ours to care for. It's also nice to have someone else do the laundry. Laundry is my least favorite chore, but Evan doesn't mind it, and as long as he uses the right detergent—I have sensitive skin—I'm not too picky.

The doorbell rings at one thirty. Since Evan is upstairs, I open the door.

"Hi," I say to Lynne and Howie. "Come in."

They step into the front hall, and I'm reminded of the fact that the last time I saw them, Lynne tried to convince me to go on a honeymoon.

Fortunately, there's no mention of that now.

"Don't worry, we won't stay long," Howie says jovially. He doesn't take off his shoes; he just stands on the front mat. "I'm sure you two newlyweds have lots of plans." He holds a large reusable bag toward me. When I grasp it, I'm momentarily caught off guard by how heavy it is.

"You shouldn't have," I say, just as Evan appears at my side.

He greets his parents with hugs. His mother hands him another bag, which looks like it's as heavy as the one in my hands.

After they leave, Evan and I unload the food in the kitchen. In addition to the containers from the restaurant, there's fruit and numerous nonperishables, almost as if they think there are no Asian grocery stores in Richmond Hill.

Ha! There's a T&T less than a ten-minute drive away, just for starters.

It's weird to think of my father randomly visiting me. Even if he lived in the Toronto area, I can't imagine it. Would my mom have done something like this?

We fill our plates with warm food and eat at the kitchen table, and then Evan goes to see his cousin. I cut the grass, text Yvonne about our new purchases, and watch a twisted psychological thriller that I know Evan has no interest in. It's a bit weird to watch a movie like this when it's light out, though it's still suitably creepy, and the shrimp chips—courtesy of his parents—are tasty.

And when the movie is over and my husband has yet to return, I realize, with a start, that I miss him. I was glad to have some time without him, but now, I wish he'd return.

A moment later, as if I've summoned him—which, to be honest, is a rather disturbing idea, given what I just watched—I hear a key in the lock, and I have to hold myself back from bounding to the door.

What's with this excessive enthusiasm? I see Evan every day. We used to go *weeks* without seeing each other, even if we'd text every few days.

Still, it seems polite to greet him, so I walk to the front door.

"How's Isobel and her family?" I ask, and he regales me with stories about Nolan, who's currently obsessed with nail polish and Batman. Evan shows me his right hand, which has some awkwardly applied black nail polish on three fingers, and I chuckle and say I'll go with him the next time he visits his cousin.

Yeah, married life is rather nice.

Sunday morning, Evan still isn't up when I finish my shower, so I start the coffeemaker, and for some reason, I find myself pouring my coffee into a mug with a cartoon rabbit. I truly don't know what's come over me; it doesn't feel *bad*, though.

But when I head outside, I check social media and my heart plummets.

You know those people you follow on social media, even though you haven't talked to them in a decade or more? Gina Bloomberg is one of those people. We were good friends in elementary school, and not so close in high school. We still got along well enough, and I remember sitting next to her in Grade 11 math, but we didn't hang out with the same people, and we didn't stay in touch after graduation.

Yet despite the distance between us, I'm not unaffected by the post announcing her mother's death.

"Is something wrong?"

I jerk my head up, remembering where I am. I'm usually very much aware of my surroundings; I wouldn't normally be startled by Evan sitting down next to me. But I was recalling that day in Shoppers, all those years ago. The sleepovers in Gina's basement.

"A friend from elementary school...her mom died." For some reason, I hold my phone toward Evan, as if he needs to see the evidence that it's true.

He wraps me in his arms. He must assume that I'm sad for someone who was once close to me, and that hearing about the loss of a mother is complicated for me.

But it's Gina's mom, so there's more to it.

"When I was in grade seven," I begin, "my relationship with my father went downhill. Well, it started earlier, actually. Maybe grade six..." I'm not terribly articulate right now, but that's okay. It's just Evan.

Except "just" seems like a silly word. I don't mean that he's inconsequential; no, I mean that I don't need to turn myself "on" around him. I've developed a new level of comfort with him, one I don't have around anyone else.

"Anyway," I say, "my dad pulled away when I started going through puberty. The changes made him even more uncomfortable than they made me. The summer before grade seven, the older sister of another friend was giving away some old clothes. When she asked if I wanted any, I took a black tube top. I didn't think at all about how it would look on me; I just thought it would be comfortable to wear in our hot house. The a/c was broken and my dad hadn't called the repair guy. But when I came downstairs wearing that shirt, he flipped out. I assured him that I had no plans to wear it outside, but he made me throw it out. Anyway." Yeah, I'm really not very articulate right now. "When I got my period near the end of grade seven, he drove me to Shoppers, gave me twenty dollars, and told me to get what I needed."

"He didn't come in with you?"

"No, he waited in the parking lot. And I was twelve, I had no fucking clue. I mean, I'd had sex ed, and I knew in theory what I needed, but there were so many options. I also felt like it was something your mother was supposed to help with. Or failing that, an older sister or aunt. I knew my dad didn't really know, but he could have at least been there with me. I felt so alone." I'd stuffed toilet paper in my underwear, and I was miserable. "I started bawling my eyes out in the feminine hygiene section, and that's when Gina's mom found me."

I've actually never told this story to anyone before, and it doesn't feel weird that I'm telling it to Evan, even if I can't look at his face as I continue.

It was obvious to Gina's mom what was happening, and she knew my mother was gone. I clearly remember she had a package of toilet paper in one hand and some soap in the other. I'm sure she had better things to do than help me, but she stood there for fifteen minutes, calmly explaining all the different products. She wasn't appalled by my changing body or upset that I was causing a scene. She also told me to ask my dad for any painkillers if I needed them. When I questioned why I'd need painkillers, she discovered that no one had ever mentioned the possibility of cramps to me. She went to another aisle and picked out a hot water bottle.

"Twenty minutes later," I say, "when I had everything I needed and wasn't quite so overwhelmed, I begged her not to say anything to Gina. Some girls might have felt comfortable with their friends knowing about such things, but not me. I was thankful, but I wanted this to be something that no one else ever knew about. She promised not to tell, and she gave me her cell number in case I had any other questions."

And I did. One other time, many months later, I had questions about bras, and she was very helpful. But when I saw her at Gina's, she never mentioned it, which I appreciated.

It was also reassuring that she clearly didn't approve of my father's actions. I felt like I had to make excuses for him because he was a man, but from her reaction, even if she didn't say much about it, I could tell she had higher expectations.

"Anyway," I say, yet again, then drain my cold coffee, "she was a mother to me when I needed it. Few people ever did something like that for me." I sob on the last word and realize I'm crying, just as I was crying that day in the drugstore.

Evan moves his chair closer to mine.

"I haven't seen Gina in fifteen years, but I could send her an email." I don't know if she still checks the email address I have for her, but if it doesn't work, I can DM her. "It wouldn't be weird if I told her a version of that story, would it? The rare times it happens, I appreciate when people have memories of my mother to share."

I know Evan understands that I will relate this story in a much different way than I told it to him. It won't include my complicated relationship with my father. And yes, Gina has decades of memories with her mother, whereas I had much less time with my own mom. But I still think it would be nice to add more than a generic expression of condolences.

"I don't know what it's like to lose a parent," he says, "but I think that would be fine. You know your friend better than I do, though, even if you haven't seen her in years."

"Will you read it for me later?"

He nods, and we sit in silence for a while as kids shriek in the distance.

"I often wonder what my dad was like with Peyton when she went through puberty," I say. "I'm not around enough to know if it changed their relationship. If Peyton didn't have a mother, I would have, um, offered my help. But she does, so I didn't say anything. It's not like we're close." I study my empty mug. "I sent the wedding photo link to my dad, and he finally responded yesterday. He said they were pretty and he's sorry he couldn't be there."

And that was it.

Well, he asked for my new address, too. Maybe he intends me to send me an impersonal card—that's all I can hope for.

I wipe my eyes with my hand, and Evan goes inside and comes back with a box of tissues. I murmur my thanks.

Why am I talking so much today? Why am I so emotional about this?

Once again, I think back to my preteen years. When I shed a few tears, it freaked my father out. I learned not to express myself around him. But Evan is fine with it. I can let down my guard around him.

I've lived with people as an adult before, but just roommates when I was in university. It's different from living with someone now, someone who's building a life with me. I feel like I made a really good choice, even if our marriage might not be "conventional."

This was another thing I struggled with as I grew up. It slowly became apparent that I didn't think about boys the way many girls did. I occasionally had minor crushes, but something about it felt different, and I didn't have the words to explain it.

Everything with sex and relationships has always been very fraught for me. For multiple reasons, yet somehow, I'm sobbing quietly in the backyard while my husband holds my hand, and it's all okay.

Except it's not. Gina's mother is dead. She couldn't have been all that old—under sixty-five, I'm guessing? Cancer, like my mom.

I feel all tangled up; I don't like being overwhelmed by my emotions. But Evan is here, and his touch grounds me. It's always been comfortable to talk to him, but before we got married, I know I wouldn't have shared all this.

I look up at him and before I know what I'm doing, I trace his jawline with my finger, while my other hand is still gripped in his. The first time I looked at his face this closely was two days ago, when I did his makeup. I feel like I never saw it, not really, until recently. I study the faint lines at the corners of his eyes, the freckle near his temple.

But this sort of touch is different from holding hands or cuddling. Worried I might have overstepped, I pull back, though we continue to sit in the backyard for a long time.

That afternoon, I sit cross-legged on my bed and draft an email to Gina on my laptop. I've written a grand total of one sentence when I start to doubt myself. Maybe her mom was one of those people who could be generous outside her home, but with her own family, it was a different matter, and my email will cause more hurt...

I don't think so, but it's been well over a decade since I talked to Gina.

The thing about death is that so many people are afraid of saying the wrong thing, and they end up saying nothing at all.

I write a couple of paragraphs, expressing my condolences and briefly describing my memories of her mother. I'm debating what to put in the subject line when Evan knocks on my door, as if he knows I'm almost finished.

"Hey." He gestures to my laptop. "Are you ready for me to read it?"

I shift over on the bed, making space for him to sit beside me. I'm a bit embarrassed by the number of tabs open in my browser—it's not like me—but I quickly shove down that feeling. It's not as if my husband is seeing me naked.

And oh my God, why am I thinking about that? It's completely inappropriate.

Evan skims what I've written. "You're missing a word here." He points to the screen.

"Right. Thank you." I'd read it over and over, but sometimes when you do that, you can't see it clearly anymore; you need a new perspective. "Is it okay otherwise?"

"Yeah. It's good."

I add a subject and send it to the email address that I used for talking to Gina on MSN Messenger, back when we were in high school. Then I close the laptop and put it aside. I lie down on my bed, and Evan hesitates before lying down next to me, his arm loosely slung over my waist. It's similar to cuddling on the couch, which we often do when we watch TV, but something about being in bed makes it seem a little different.

I feel a prickle of guilt. Evan should have more; he should have love.

Instead, he has me.

Chapter 12

Evan

"Is it hot in here, or is it just me?" I ask on Wednesday, as Jane and I eat lunch together.

I wince. Did that sound dirty?

"I mean, do you think the a/c is working?" I amend. I'm sweating, and while I'm particularly prone to sweating, I'm usually comfortable inside our house, which is set at 23°C; the basement, where I work, is a couple of degrees cooler.

Jane sets down her chopsticks. "Yeah, you're right. It's a bit warm." She gets up.

"You don't have to..." My voice trails off. She's already at the thermostat.

"It's twenty-six in here."

Shit. After the morning I've had, the thought of figuring this out is a little too much.

Jane heads to the basement, where the heat pump is located. I finish my last few bites of lunch and join her.

"What's wrong?" I ask, though I don't expect her to have an answer.

She shrugs. "You go back to work, and I'll worry about this."

"Are you sure?"

"Absolutely."

I return to my basement office, which is blessedly cooler than the kitchen, and I've spent about twenty minutes answering emails when there's a knock on the door of my office.

"Come in," I say.

Jane appears in the doorway. "I tried a bunch of things I found online, but nothing worked. So, I called a local repair guy. He's on vacation, but the second company I called can come tomorrow morning."

I know this is all stuff I could do myself. However, it's nice to have someone else take care of it. I would have gotten anxious, wondered why the hell I thought I was ready for home ownership, then beaten myself up for freaking out.

"Thank you," I say. "I really appreciate it."

Do I sound too grateful? I don't know. But it's better than taking Jane for granted.

We decide it's too hot to cuddle while watching our K-drama that evening, but with a fan, I manage to sleep okay, and the doorbell rings at 11 a.m. Though it's quickly followed by the sound of Jane's footsteps on the stairs, I figure I should go up, too.

I arrive just as Jane opens the door to a white man in his fifties. When he asks what the problem is, he looks directly at me. Because I'm the man of the household, I guess.

However, when she answers, he immediately redirects his attention and further questions to her, and she leads him to the basement. I debate whether to stay with them, but Jane looks comfortable enough handling this, so I head to my office, though I keep the door open.

Fifteen minutes later, she appears at my door and names something that needs to be replaced, which he's doing right now. It doesn't mean anything to me, but it's apparently three hundred dollars, and everything will be operational again soon, which is the important part. While I cringe a little at the price, it could have been so much worse. Besides, we've budgeted for repairs like this.

And Jane really does look nice in that blue V-neck T-shirt and jeans shorts. Her skin glistens with sweat, and I think it would also be nice to see her sweating beneath me...

No! Why am I thinking about that?

I scrub a hand over my face.

"Evan?" she says. "Is that okay with you?"

"Yes." I clear my throat. "Of course."

My attraction to Jane is really becoming a problem, and I swear my heart skips a beat in the silliest of situations. Like when she found Watson sitting in her chair at dinnertime, and the left corner of her mouth curled up. Just a little thing, but I'm still thinking about it twenty-four hours later.

And thinking about other things involving her mouth.

The night after the heat pump is repaired, we return to cuddling while we watch the K-drama, but I miss a bunch of dialogue because I'm too busy focusing on her skin against mine to read the subtitles—and too embarrassed to ask to go back. Fortunately, she rarely wants to discuss the episode afterward. I'd make a fool of myself if she did.

Ugh. This wasn't supposed to happen. But the combination of her capability and composure—plus her occasional vulnerability—is getting to me.

The next day at dinner, she tells me that Gina emailed her back. She hadn't really expected a response from her childhood friend, even if she still checked that email address semi-regularly, but Gina seemed happy to hear from her. There's a strange look on Jane's face, which I read as fond sadness, and it stirs more unwanted feelings in me.

Yeah, I cannot be alone with this woman all weekend.

When we're cleaning up, I say, "How about we have Max and Kim over for a meal?"

"You're an idiot," I mutter to myself as Jane enters the kitchen, wearing dark jeans and the black shirt that she wore on our date last week.

"What's that?" she asks.

"Nothing!" I say. "Nothing at all."

"It sounded like you were talking to the cheese." She gestures to the cheese board that I'm in the middle of preparing. We're making good use of our friends' housewarming gift.

"Maybe I was," I say playfully.

This is, of course, better than telling her the truth: I was cursing myself for giving her a reason to dress up a little. Why do I find her exposed collarbone so enticing?

She ties my flowered apron around her waist, and that doesn't help. There's something endearingly incongruous about her outfit.

My older brother and his girlfriend are coming for an early Saturday dinner, and we're doing burgers on the barbecue. And by "we," I mean Jane, who's more excited about grilling than me, though I was the one who procured the barbecue. I bought it secondhand from someone down the street. They'd gotten a fancy new barbecue and didn't need this one anymore. It cost me fifty bucks. I have no expectation that it'll last for a long time, but I hope we can get a year or two out of it.

The doorbell rings.

"I'll get it." I wash my hands, exit the kitchen, and open the front door. "Welcome to our air-conditioned house!"

Kim smiles and gives me a quick hug. "Hey, Evan."

She and Max have been together about year, which is the same amount of time that Jane and I have supposedly been together. They met at their friends' wedding, then proceeded to see each other at a bunch of other weddings that summer.

"How was the drive?" I ask.

"Not bad," my brother says. He's standing behind Kim and has a bakery box in his hand. He looks a little stern, but there's nothing unusual about that.

Kim tugs him inside, and my gaze is riveted on that point of contact. Though Jane might touch my hand, I know for them, it's a sign of something more. I can't help feeling envious of Max. Before, it was a general feeling of envy—he had a serious romantic relationship and I didn't—but now, I have a particular person in mind.

Jane Yin.

And the preposterous thing is that we're already married.

I clear my throat. "What did you bring for dessert?" I ask as Max hands me the box.

"A very sophisticated cake," Kim replies.

"It's an affront to human decency," Max says.

She gives him a playful shove before putting on a pair of slippers from the collection by the door.

"You've piqued my curiosity." I lead the way to the kitchen, where I set the box next to the cheese board on the table. "Should I take a look now?"

"Absolutely not," my brother says. "I'm embarrassed to be in the same room as it." But a smile tugs at his lips.

"Would you like anything to drink?" Jane asks. "Beer, wine, juice, tea, water?" She puts aside the salad bowl and walks over to our guests.

"I'll have a glass of wine if you've got a bottle open, but no need to open one on my account," Kim says.

"Don't worry, I want some, too." Jane takes out a bottle of red and pours small glasses for her, Max, and Kim. "Help yourself to the cheese."

Kim immediately reaches for a piece of gouda, her eagerness eliciting chuckles. Once she and Max have had something to eat, I offer them a tour while Jane gets started on the barbecue.

I begin with the kitchen. "As you can see, we have a selection of thirty-year-old appliances."

"Probably for the best," Max says. "The new ones don't last."

I move to the living room. "This is our mass cane plant, which has been with us for eight days. And Watson, who will probably be too shy to say hello."

"I love your couch," Kim says.

"That was Jane's." I nod at my wife as she heads out back with the raw burgers. "She had it in her apartment." Mine, which isn't as nice, is currently in the basement.

I proceed through the rest of the downstairs, trying to see how the house would look to someone who doesn't live here. We're still missing a dining room table, and the décor is a bit sparse. I'm not sure it truly looks *homey* yet, but it's starting to feel that way to me.

Though that's partly due to the woman who just cursed on our back patio.

"You okay?" I ask.

"Yeah," she says. "I dropped a bun on the grass, that's all."

I continue the tour, Kim asking more questions than Max. I don't offer to show them the second floor, and fortunately, neither of them asks. I'm not sure what my brother would think of the separate bedrooms.

When we return to the kitchen, I move the cheese board to the counter and set out plates. A moment later, Jane enters with platters of beef patties and toasted buns. Some of her hair has escaped her ponytail. She sets everything down, then removes her apron. Even though she's barely showing more skin than before, seeing her take off an article of clothing—even with family here—makes my blood pump faster.

I try to ignore that feeling. "Help yourself. I'll bring the salad over in a minute."

I go to the counter and toss the green salad with the vinai-grette. I'm about to reach for the salad tongs when I feel a warm hand on my lower back, and I'm so shocked, I jump back, knocking against Jane.

"Sorry! You surprised me," I say, even though we touch each other like that regularly.

The problem? I'd just been thinking about her taking off clothes, which is highly inappropriate, and when she touched me, it felt like something more than our usual physical contact.

As I steady my breathing and set the salad tongs in the bowl, I note that Max's eyes have narrowed suspiciously, as if asking, *Why does a touch from your wife shock you so much?*

I ignore him and take the salad to the table. "Bon appétit."

"I think it's finally time to see what's in this box." I bring over plates and clean utensils for dessert.

"Don't say I didn't warn you," Max mutters.

I remove the tape and open up the box to reveal...a giant burger. Except it doesn't contain any meat or meat substitute.

No, it's a burger cake. Not a super realistic one that you might actually mistake for a hamburger, but it's clearly supposed to be a burger.

"This looks amazing," I say, in part to annoy my brother.

"The middle cake is chocolate," Kim says. "The cakes that form the bun are vanilla. The condiments are made of different colors of buttercream."

"Uh, wow. Yes." Jane seems a little perturbed that this is sitting in our kitchen.

"You see?" Max turns to me. "Jane agrees that it's an abomination."

She looks at Kim. "I really do apprec—"

Kim waves this off. "It's fine. We're family now. You're allowed to disapprove of the cake I chose. I do think it'll taste good, even if the aesthetics aren't to your preference."

Jane opens her mouth, but no words come out. I suspect it's because she's processing Kim's casual mention of "family," and I figure a distraction is in order, in case she needs a few moments to compose herself.

"I think Watson would like to try the cake," I say.

Max merely raises an eyebrow, but at least he's not looking at Jane. Though he might think I'm joking, I really mean it. After all, Watson was unable to partake in our earlier burgers and is feeling left out.

The cake sits on a piece of cardboard inside the box. Carefully, I pick it up, set it on a large plate, and walk over to where Watson is standing beneath the mass cane plant. He has difficulty holding a fork, so I set the fork on the plate and take a picture as Kim laughs.

When I return the cake to the table, Jane is ready to cut it with a knife.

"Would you like a piece, Max?" she asks.

"A cake should look like a cake, not whatever this is. But I suppose I have to try it."

Ha. Unlike Leo, Max would never turn down cake, but he sounds incredibly put out by this state of affairs.

Jane serves us each a slice, and I try a forkful with both bun and meat.

"It's delicious," I tell Kim, and that's not a lie—it's a pretty decent cake, even if it's not as good as our wedding cake. "Thank you for bringing it."

She nods before turning to Jane. "So, how's living in the suburbs and having a mother- and father-in-law?"

"I rarely leave the house anyway," Jane says, "and to be honest..." She pauses. I'm not sure what she wants to share, and I'm ready to jump in at any moment, but she soon continues, her voice steady. "I wanted to have more family. My mom is dead, and my dad lives out west and didn't bother to come to the wedding, as you probably noticed. So, I thought I..."

I squeeze her hand under the table.

"Shit, I'm sorry," Kim says. "I admit that being part of another person's family was the part I dreaded most about a long-term relationship"—she glances at Max—"but of course, not everyone is like me."

"Your parents are nice," Jane says to Max. "They don't intrude on our lives too much."

"Other than the honeymoon thing," Kim says.

"Yeah. Other than that." My wife manages a wry chuckle. "Maybe they're trying to give us lots of time alone to make grandchildren."

Max and I simultaneously choke on our cake. I didn't expect to hear Jane say *that* in company, and it doesn't help that she looks so lovely in her black shirt, her lips twitching as she calmly brings another bite of cake to her mouth. When I continue to hack away, she puts a hand on my back—and this time, I don't startle.

"Sorry," she murmurs. "You okay?"

"Yeah, just...peachy," I say, but the thought of the baby-making process with Jane has gotten too appealing. Plus, the thought of any sexual activity that might not lead to a baby. Like...

I will myself to picture something else. Anything else. Deciding I should go big, I think of whales, but that makes me think of *sperm* whales. Though I have no idea what they look like, that word isn't helping.

I shove another bite of cake in my mouth and manage not to choke—barely. Perhaps my brother is right. This cake is cursed.

He gives me an odd look, and I try to smile.

I wonder what he thinks of my marriage now.

"The burgers turned out well," Jane says as we clean up afterward.

"They did." I lower the remnants of the burger cake into a container. When I get some yellow buttercream on my finger, my first instinct is to ask her to lick it off, but I shove down that temptation and lick my own finger.

"Was I...okay?" she asks, uncertainty in her voice.

I glance up. "What do you mean?"

"We've never spent time with just Max and Kim before. I don't want to ask if they liked me—it sounds childish—but maybe I shouldn't have made that crack about grandchildren?"

"No, no, that was fine."

"Once or twice, I've gotten the feeling that Max is still suspicious of me. Does he think I'm not good enough for you?"

I hate hearing her say that.

I close the distance between us. "He definitely doesn't, but he isn't sure what to make of our relationship because everything happened so fast."

She sighs and scrubs a hand over her face. "I don't want to cause any problems between you and your brothers."

"You're not causing problems. Things will return to normal soon." Though me jumping back when Jane touched me may not have helped.

"You can tell him the truth, if he can keep a secret."

"He can. But I won't." A part of me wants to tell my older brother, but I feel like he wouldn't understand, and he'd be concerned that I gave up on love.

But as I look at Jane now, worrying her bottom lip with her teeth...

I did expect our relationship to change a little once we got married and started spending more time together. A deepening of our friendship, so to speak.

Except my feelings aren't platonic now. No, some part of me aches for a romance—with her. There's a sexual component to it, sure, but it's not simply lust.

"Is everything okay?" she asks, a notch of concern appearing between her eyebrows.

She's gotten better at reading me over the past month. Or I've gotten worse at pasting on a smile and pretending everything's okay around her.

"Yeah," I tell her. "I'm good."

After all, I'm married to an amazing woman, aren't I?

Chapter 13

Jane

It starts on Monday morning, which is terrible timing.

After my shower, I come downstairs and find Evan sitting on the carpet by the back door. He's still working on positioning Watson and a friend. Yes, it appears that our penguin now has company in the form of a plush green frog. Evan puts the small frog on Watson's head.

"Stay still," he says.

The frog promptly falls off.

However, Evan's next attempt is successful. His lips quirk up as he turns toward me, and I feel an unfamiliar spark in my body.

My husband is wearing shorts and a white T-shirt, nothing I haven't seen him wear many times before. He's also wearing his glasses.

Why do I find this ridiculously charming? And why am I mesmerized by the sight of his arm? His hand, as he pushes himself up from the floor. They're just body parts, and yet...

I think I'm experiencing physical attraction?

"Your coffee's outside," he says.

For a few seconds, my feet are rooted to the floor, but then I retreat to the table out back, where the caffeine-and-chaos mug is waiting for me. That seems fitting since my feelings are rather chaotic right now.

"How's your workweek looking?" Evan asks.

I'm weirdly entranced by his lips. Why is this happening? Why am I imagining those lips around my nipple?

"Um. Not too bad," I say. "Yours?"

I maintain some semblance of a conversation for the next few minutes, but I keep being distracted by the stupidest things, and when Evan smiles, I swear I can *feel* it inside me.

Having coffee together outside is usually a pleasant, comfortable way to start the day. But now, it feels anything but comfortable, and I don't want him to know. I'm relieved when I'm able to escape to my office upstairs—two full floors away from Evan—and turn on my work computer. Hopefully that experience was temporary, and when I see him again at lunch, I'll be back to normal. The only times I've felt sexual attraction, I was in love, and that's only happened twice.

I'm not in love with Evan, am I?

No. Not in the way I was with my exes. But we see so much of each other, and we're building a life together. I guess that connection is causing this. It certainly isn't something I expected in my marriage.

Is it happening to Evan, too?

I shake my head, as if the movement will dismiss that thought from my head. It's probably just me.

It takes several minutes, but eventually, I'm able to get my mind away from thoughts of my husband's arms and lips—seriously, what's wrong with me?—and focus on my job.

At noon, I'm still not ready to see Evan, so I send him a text telling him to eat without me because I want to finish my current task. I hear him moving around downstairs, and just after twelve thirty, which is when he usually returns to work, I head to the kitchen. I haven't heard any noises in a few minutes, so I hope he's back in the basement.

However, it appears that hope was in vain because I crash into him in the hallway while lost in my thoughts.

"Sorry!" I say.

He sets his hand on my waist to steady me. Nothing he hasn't done many times before, but this time, it feels different. I don't think *he's* doing anything differently; no, my body is just over-sensitized. When he retreats to his office, I finally feel like I can breathe again.

How do people deal with this nonsense?

By the time we finish dinner, the weirdness of earlier has mostly disappeared. After work, Evan went for a walk and came back a little sweaty, and I didn't think anything of it, like usual.

Really, it was just like usual. I swear!

As we clean up, I'm extra careful not to accidentally knock into him, afraid it'll start an unwanted avalanche of thoughts and feelings.

But when we start watching an episode of our current K-drama, I allow myself to snuggle against him. This is how we usually watch TV, and it would be suspicious if I didn't, right?

We're two friends being platonically affectionate, that's all. Nothing more to it than that. It's something we both enjoy, and we agreed on this before we got married.

At one point, Evan shifts, and his shirt rides up. My fingers brush bare skin, and I can't help my swift intake of breath, which he hopefully doesn't notice.

What if I slid my hand up higher, under his shirt, over the smooth extent of his back?

Okay, this is getting out of control. As soon as we finish this episode, I'm going to get myself off. With any luck, once I take care of my needs, these thoughts will stop.

They do not stop.

The next day, when Evan is out for a walk, I call Claudia without texting her first.

"Hey," I say when she picks up. I suddenly remember that since she's three hours behind us, she's probably still working. "Can you talk right now? Just for a few minutes."

Her brows crease in concern. "What's up?"

"I think I'm attracted to Evan."

Claudia, at least, will understand how weird this is for me—and besides, she's the only one who knows the truth about our marriage. There's no one else I can tell.

"What happened?" she asks.

"Yesterday morning, he was just sitting there! On the floor! Beside Watson—"

"Wait, who's Watson?"

"A giant plush penguin. He lives in our living room, and Evan dresses him up every day. Like, with a hat or a lei. Anyway, he was sitting next to Watson, and I thought he was kind of sexy. Ugh."

"Do you actually want something to happen? Sexually, I mean. Or would you prefer to admire him from a distance?"

"My body wants something to happen," I admit miserably. "It makes everything *so* confusing and complicated. I wasn't supposed to be attracted to my husband."

Claudia chuckles.

"What?" I'm on edge.

"It sounds funny when you say it like that. Most people are attracted to their spouses."

"And most people don't make marriage pacts during a pandemic, but here I am."

"Well, what are the options?" she asks.

"I could tell him and he could reject me. Super awkward because we live together."

"Or he could...not reject you."

"I have no evidence he feels that way." I pause. "Though to be fair, I'm sometimes clueless when it comes to such things. I don't always notice."

My skin heats at the thought of telling him, his slow smile as he kisses me...

"Besides," I say, pushing aside that silly fantasy, "we've kissed. At the wedding, for starters—"

"When else did you kiss?"

"As, um, practice. Anyway, it didn't do anything for me, though maybe it would be different now. Does that often happen? I have no idea."

"You're talking to *me*," she says.

"Right. Yeah." I just don't know what to do. When the air conditioner stopped working, I sprang into action and managed it, and I didn't mind. There was a clear problem to be solved, unlike now. Nothing seems clear.

"Is part of the issue," she says gently, "that whenever this has happened in the past, you were in love?"

Yeah. Because, like sex, this sort of love wasn't in my plans. I'd given up on it.

"Why is it so complicated?" I mutter. "I don't love him like that, but I can feel stuff...changing."

"Sometimes people fall in love after they get married."

"But in those cases, they don't usually know each other well beforehand, right? I met Evan over a decade ago." I sigh. "What should I do?"

"This just started, right? Wait a few days and see if it lasts. Or if it changes."

"Yes. That's sensible. Sorry for talking about this so much."

She waves this off. "What else is new with you?"

"Um, Max and Kim"—Claudia met them at the wedding—"came over, and they brought a cake shaped like a burger. Well, Kim picked it out. Max thought it looked appalling."

"Do you like having in-laws?"

"Yeah, I kind of do. His parents brought a hundred dollars' worth of food over the other weekend."

She laughs. "So, you're using them for food?"

"No! It's not the monetary value; it's having family who thinks of you enough to do such things. What it stands for." It sounds cheesy when I put it like that, and I know they were thinking more of Evan than me. But still.

I'd heard of parents giving their adult children things they didn't need, but it wasn't something I experienced myself. Asian friends, in particular, might talk about how their parents were always trying to feed them and would bring food rather than saying "I love you."

Both were completely outside my experience.

Somehow, the conversation segues into Claudia complaining about one of her coworkers. She says that when she mentioned this story to her sister, her sister suggested they go out, and Claudia rolled her eyes so hard that she feared she might have damaged them.

When I hear the front door open, I jump.

"Is Evan home?" she asks.

"Uh. Yeah."

I feel embarrassed, even though we weren't talking about him anymore. And Evan returning after a walk is an everyday occurrence. He'll be sweaty, and he'll have a shower...

Oh God. Thinking about him in the shower is just making it worse.

I try to scrub my brain of those thoughts. I'll finish this conversation, then go downstairs and cook dinner. Nothing I haven't done many times before.

It'll be okay.

It's not okay.

Evan comes downstairs after I've finished making pesto in the food processor. His hair is slightly damp.

"Did you use our basil?" He tilts his head in the direction of our backyard, and why am I admiring his neck?

Stupid brain.

"Uh, yes," I say. "Could you cook the pasta while I barbecue the chicken? I have boneless thighs, so it won't take long."

"Sure thing." He smiles.

Ugh, why does he have to do that?

"Did you say something?" he asks.

Oh no. Did I mutter that under my breath?

"Nope!" I grab the chicken out of the fridge—I applied a dry rub before my call with Claudia—and escape out the back door.

My skin is warm and prickly, but I feel a bit better once the chicken is underway. It really is nice to be able to grill in the backyard.

While my attraction to Evan seems like it came out of nowhere, I know that's not the case. I know *something* has been happening for a while now, thanks to the thoughtful shit he does. Every weekday, he makes me coffee and dresses up a giant plushie—the penguin is currently wearing a red beret. He's gotten us patio furniture and a barbecue without spending much money, and without me having to lift a finger. He's also…

I have to stop making a list. It's not helping. Maybe these things sound mundane, but I feel like I'm being cared for on a daily basis, which is a luxury.

I flip over the chicken.

"Jane?" Evan appears at the back door.

"What?" I snap.

He looks taken aback by my tone, and something clenches in my chest.

"Sorry," I say, setting down the tongs.

He steps onto the patio, and even though I'm prepared for him to put his hand on my shoulder, it still shocks me. When he strokes his thumb over my skin—I'm wearing a tank top—it's almost too much. I want to burrow into him and run away at the same time, but I force myself to do neither.

"Sorry," I say again. "I, um. I was lost in my thoughts. Did you have a question?"

"Mm. That smells good." He nods toward the barbecue. "What did you want on the salad? Oil and vinegar?"

"Yep. Just something simple." I smile to show him that everything is normal with me, but I must overdo it because he gives me an odd look.

As he heads back inside, I think of his words.

Oil and vinegar.

They don't mix.

But that's not a good comparison for us. Sure, our personalities are rather different, but we're similar in many ways, and we've been cohabitating in relative harmony for several weeks.

I use an instant-read thermometer to check if the chicken is ready. When it reaches the desired temperature, I take the thighs off the grill and bring them inside. Evan has everything dished out: the salad in small bowls, the pasta on plates. He's in the process of grating the parmesan.

"Thanks for taking care of the pasta," I say as I set two thighs on each plate. It's little things like this, I think, that are helping our marriage work. Showing appreciation for each other.

I have to remind myself not to screw up what we have.

After dinner, I'm more excited about watching a show than I should be. I tell myself it's because I want to see what will happen, but I know that's not the only reason.

I take a seat on the couch, on the opposite side from Evan. He turns to me and tilts his head, a question in his eyes.

"It's warm in here," I say.

"Do you want me to turn down the thermostat?"

"No, that's okay."

We're on the eighth of sixteen episodes. This particular drama is a romance with a fake engagement, interfering parents, and a chaebol. It's rather similar to the last one we watched, truth be told, but there's something comforting in that.

As the camera zooms in on the hero's fingers brushing the heroine's, I have a terrible premonition. They're finally going to kiss in this episode, aren't they?

"Have you cooled down?" Evan asks.

I jerk my head away from the screen and realize his face is right...there. Without being aware of what I was doing, I cuddled up against him.

It would feel weird to pull back now, so I say, "Um. Yeah."

Onscreen, the heroine trips and falls into the hero's lap. Her lips are a hair's breadth from his, and they look into each other's eyes for what feels like eternity but is probably just a few seconds.

Is this it? Are they going to...?

I can hardly breathe.

And when Evan shifts against me, I become unbearably aware of him. His side against mine. His hand resting on my waist.

The heroine steps back, and I nearly growl in frustration. Evan releases a huff of amusement—at me, or the antics of the people onscreen? I don't know, but the rumble of his chest is almost too much for me.

Maybe if I had more experience with these sorts of feelings, I wouldn't be having such difficulties, but being attracted to someone for the first time in more than nine years is really doing a number on me.

I use all my willpower to focus on the screen rather than the man beside me.

A couple of minutes later, the heroine is having yet another argument with her mom. She leaves in a huff, and I'm both pleased and annoyed when she hightails it out of there and finds the hero waiting for her. He's leaning against a sleek black car right outside the house. They exchange a few words, and his hand hovers above her cheek for an infuriatingly long time. When his thumb brushes her skin, I'm filled with anticipation. His head dips closer, but still not close enough, and then...and then...

Onscreen, his lips meet hers, and I swear Evan's hand tightens around my waist. It's the smallest of movements, and if I wasn't so attuned to his body, I probably wouldn't notice.

But I do.

The next thing I know, I've launched myself on top of him. He's on his back now, his head resting on the arm of the couch. For a moment, it's like time stops—and then my lips crash down on his.

It's completely different from the other times we kissed, which seem oh-so-long ago now. I'm not thinking about individual body parts this time. No, I'm relieved and exhilarated.

Because he's kissing me back.

It doesn't feel like it's simply an instinctive reaction to having someone else's lips on his. I don't know how to explain it, but it feels like it matters that it's *my* lips.

When he shifts to the side, my heart sinks. Oh God, he's realized what he's doing and...

He sets his glasses on the coffee table and returns to kissing me, his arms encircling my back. I smile in relief against his lips. Experimentally, I touch my tongue against his. He makes a soft moan in the back of his throat, unlike any sound I've heard from him before. It spurs me on. I slide a hand into his hair and tug lightly; he likes that, too.

Evan and I have spent a ton of time together lately, but there are so many things that we haven't done, and I desperately want to do them all. It's wonderful to have an outlet for all the feelings swirling around in me. I can't put anything into words right now, but kissing? I can manage that.

He squirms against me, and when I feel his erection against my thigh, I freeze. It's such an unfamiliar sensation. I mean, this is all so unfamiliar, but for some reason, that's what reminds me of what I'm doing.

I'm having a hot make-out session with my husband, and this was never part of the deal. Casual touches, a kiss on the forehead—sure. But not this.

I look down at Evan, slightly disheveled below me on the couch. His glasses off, his hair mussed, his lips kiss-swollen. I want to see those lips between my legs, before he...

I glance at the TV, where the show is still playing. Actually, I think it jumped to the next episode. Why are they in the woods? What happened? I have no idea.

"I have to go to the washroom," I say, then run upstairs before he can speak.

I stay in my room so I don't see Evan again that evening. At eleven thirty, as usual, I turn out the light, but nothing else about this seems usual.

I kissed him.

He kissed me back.

And it made me want him, physically, even more than before.

Has he been with anyone else since we got married? He's allowed to do that, but I find myself hating the idea. I'm not sure when he'd have the time, though. On weekdays, he rarely goes out, except for his walks—though it's possible he's hooking up with a neighbor, I suppose. On the weekends, I always know what he's doing if he's not with me.

I toss and turn, all sorts of confusing thoughts racing through my mind.

Eventually, at one in the morning, I flip on the light and read negative reviews of classic novels in an attempt to distract myself. I'm about to turn out my light again when I hear Evan moving about. Is he unable to sleep, too?

My body gets foolishly excited at the thought of him coming to my room and continuing what we started earlier, though I know he won't do that. He probably just got up to use the washroom.

But I don't hear the toilet flush.

The next morning, I push myself harder than usual on the elliptical machine, despite getting only three hours of sleep.

When I head back downstairs after my shower, the coffee is done but not poured, and Watson is wearing the same red beret as yesterday. Such little things, yet fear creeps up my spine. This isn't our usual weekday routine.

Did I break my marriage?

Chapter 14

Evan

WHEN I RETURN DOWNSTAIRS, I remove the beret from Watson's head and put some Mardi Gras beads around his neck. I look up and note with a jolt that Jane is already outside, mug in hand. Owing to my poor night's sleep, I was a little late getting out of bed this morning, but she's outside at the same time as usual, and I feel guilty that she had to pour her coffee.

After grabbing a mug, I head to the backyard and take a seat. "Good morning."

She sips her coffee and gives me a nod.

"I'm sorry," I say.

"I can get my own coffee. It's fine." Her voice has a strange edge to it, and I swear there are dark circles under her eyes, even if she still looks lovely. I try not to stare at the lips that I kissed last night.

When I apologized, was it about the coffee or about something else? I don't even know.

I mean, I'm not exactly sorry about kissing her back...unless she regrets the whole thing. Then I'm sorry. But I don't know what's happening, and she doesn't give me any insight. This is the first time I've seen her since she ran upstairs nearly twelve hours ago.

That kiss...

It was nothing like the one on our wedding day. She threw herself at me while we were watching TV, and as stunned as I was, I still kissed her back immediately, my body reacting to something I'd wanted for weeks. The press of her chest against mine. The eagerness of her lips and tongue as she tried to get closer and closer. But when I bucked my hips against hers, she seemed to realize what we were doing and left.

I'm still not entirely sure why it happened, though. Was she overcome by the sexual tension onscreen? That, in itself, seems insufficient.

Does she want me? Has she been thinking about it as much as I have? Something has seemed a little off in the last couple of days, but it could be unrelated. It could have to do with Claudia—I know they spoke for a while yesterday, and they don't talk on the phone all that often.

No, I can't let myself hope, especially when she looks distraught. I'm afraid that if I try to talk about it, she'll freak out again, so I think the best course of action is to pretend we never kissed. We have to live together, after all.

The feel of her on top of me...I'll just think about that when I'm alone.

"Watson apologizes for not being ready for coffee." I gesture at him. "He was partying late last night."

Her lips curve into a cautious smile. There were a couple of times this week when her smiles seemed awkward and forced, but this seems genuine, if a little uncertain.

You see, Jane? It's okay. I'm still your friend-slash-husband.

"Any plans for the day?" she asks. "The usual?"

"Actually," I say, "my mom texted me after we...you know. She wants me to come over to move some things and have dinner, if that's okay."

"Of course."

Does she sound glad to be rid of me? I think so, but I'm scared to ask. She'd probably refute it anyway.

While I have a decent amount of experience with kissing and relationships, nothing has quite prepared me for this.

My mom regards me inquisitively from across the table. "Are you eating enough?"

"What do you mean? I'm eating lots! You keep putting food on my plate, and I'm eating it all." To emphasize this, I pick up another piece of beef.

We're sitting in the kitchen of my childhood home, after I helped my parents move some furniture in the basement. My father is to my left, between me and Mom.

She clucks her tongue. "I don't mean right now. I mean in general. Why are you so hungry tonight? Because you aren't eating enough at home?"

I'm half-afraid she's going to accuse Jane of not feeding me, even though that doesn't sound like my mother. Sure, Jane does more cooking than I do, but I'm capable of feeding myself, and my parents are aware of that. They made sure we all learned to cook.

"I didn't eat much at lunch because I wasn't hungry then," I say, "but I guess I worked up an appetite."

"Why weren't you hungry earlier?" Dad asks. "Is something wrong?"

My wife and I kissed for the first time since the wedding and everything is weird now.

"No," I say, then stuff some bok choy in my mouth.

"Maybe you're working too hard," Mom says. "You should really go on that honeymoon. It will be good for you."

"We don't need a honeymoon, and my marriage is fine."

"I didn't suggest it wasn't."

No, she didn't, not exactly, but I can feel her concern—different from her usual concern about me. The fact that I sound so defensive probably isn't helping. I'm not normally like this with my parents.

"We'll go next year," I say with a sigh.

"You can take another trip next year," Dad says. "A honeymoon should be within a few months of the wedding."

"Why are you so keen on the honeymoon?" I ask.

My parents exchange a look. They've been married for forty years, and sometimes, it feels like they can have entire conversations without speaking.

"I just think it's a nice thing to do," he says at last.

Hm. Clearly my parents don't want to say exactly what they're thinking, and I'm too scared to demand they tell me.

I'm still not in a great mood when I head to the car, leftovers and half a dozen egg tarts in a bag. I'm looking forward to seeing Jane and dreading it at the same time.

When I get home, I put everything in the fridge. Since she's not downstairs, I text her to say that I'm going for a walk and there are egg tarts if she wants one.

I don't get a response.

I return from my walk to find my wife standing at the counter, eating a tart. A crumb clings to her bottom lip, and I itch to brush it off with my finger—or lick it with my tongue—but I stuff my hands in my pockets instead.

"How are your parents?" she asks.

"The usual," I say. "They bugged me more about the honeymoon, but..." I shrug. "Nothing I can't handle."

"Are they suspicious that we...you know..."

"I'm not sure what they think now." I sigh. "I'm going to have a shower."

"Want to watch a show afterward?"

I study her. Is she trying to act like everything is normal between us? Since we usually watch a show after dinner, it would make sense that we do it now. Or is she thinking of our kiss?

I can't read her.

I said I was going to have a shower—and I will—but I could use an egg tart first. After all, I didn't have dessert at my parents' house. I take one out of the fridge, then push it out of the metal tin and set it on a small plate.

Jane promptly picks it up and pretends to take a big bite.

She doesn't normally do things like this. I step toward her, wanting my egg tart back, but she moves backward until she hits the counter. The tart—my tart—is still held aloft in her left hand. I reach for it, but she moves it over her head.

Ha! She's shorter than me, but I have to be careful so it doesn't fall on the floor.

"Why did you do it?' I ask.

She tenses. "Do what?"

"Pretend to eat my egg tart."

She visibly relaxes at those words but keeps the tart above her head.

I take another step closer. My body is flush with hers now, and she doesn't look quite so relaxed. She's breathing heavily, and the look in her eyes—I think it's excitement? I swear something is buzzing in the air between us.

I reach up and gently pry the tart from her fingers. As I take a big bite with lots of custard, some flakes of pastry fall to the tile floor. I'll clean those up later, once I've finished the tart and Jane is no longer avidly watching my lips.

"Okay," I say.

"Okay, what?"

"We can watch a show. After I shower."

When I enter the living room, the show is loaded on the screen, and Jane is seated in the middle of the couch. I take my usual seat on the left-hand side, and she presses play. This is the episode that started while we were making out yesterday, but she's gone back to the beginning of it, since neither of us was paying attention.

I feel the absence of her at my side, but I don't mention it. If she—

She shifts so she's next to me and rests her head on my shoulder, and yes, this feels right. I try to focus on the subtitles, though it's difficult. We haven't talked about our kiss, but something has changed between us. I feel like we can't go back, even if we never speak of it—and Jane doesn't seem inclined to talk about it.

But things have also changed between the characters on-screen, and when, halfway through the episode, they kiss once more, I can't help looking at Jane. She lifts her head from my shoulder, and her lips are temptingly parted. I try to raise an eyebrow in question, though I think I end up raising both instead.

And then she does something incredible: she picks up the remote and pauses the show.

My gaze drifts to the TV before turning back to her. Yesterday, I made out with my wife, and I've been thinking of little else since. My pulse thunders.

Once again, she makes the first move. When her lips meet mine, my eyes flutter closed. I didn't expect her to want this when we got married, but there's no doubt that she really does want it. And today, God help me, she settles herself on my lap and straddles me, her lips never leaving mine, as though she can't bear for them to part. She seems certain of what she wants, but I can't forget that she bolted yesterday.

Her mouth is soft and insistent, and she runs her tongue along the seam of my lips; I open for her, and she moans. I desperately want to remove her clothes and run my hands all over her skin, but I'm not sure she wishes to go that far.

Then I feel her hands creeping under the hem of my shirt, and the next thing I know, she's pushed it up to my armpits. I jerk my head toward the door, but the blinds are closed, thank God.

"Sorry," she says. "I thought...but I shouldn't..."

"No, no." I tighten my arms around her. I don't want her to go anywhere. "It's good. It's all good." I rest my hands on the bottom of her shirt, and when she nods, I whip it over her head.

Since she isn't wearing a bra, her breasts are visible to me now. I palm them. Her nipples harden, and she arches her neck and shuts her eyes. Emboldened, I kiss her neck and make my way downward, until I pull one of those hardened peaks into my mouth. She hisses out a breath and grinds herself against me.

"Fuck," I whisper.

I set my mouth back on her lips as I press my chest against hers. Every additional hiss and moan she makes is intoxicating. This is a side of Jane I've never seen before, and I can't help wanting more.

"Should we go upstairs?' I ask, trailing a hand down her back.

"*Yes.*"

Chapter 15

Jane

"Your bedroom or mine?" Evan asks at the top of the stairs.

"Yours." I'm not sure why, but I don't want to do it in my bed.

He takes my hand and leads me into his room.

I can't believe it. I'm going to have sex with my husband.

This was certainly not what I had in mind when I woke up this morning, nor when I went downstairs after my shower and found Watson wearing the exact same outfit as yesterday. No, I feared I'd fucked up, and I was determined to put it all behind me and never speak of it.

But I couldn't.

Seriously, how do people stand it? The man I want lives with me, and it's hard to ignore, and eventually, I decided I couldn't keep it up, not when he's clearly willing.

I can't think about what this all means and how it will change our relationship; I can't think at all when he removes his glasses and pulls his shirt over his head. I run my hands over his lean chest, and he drops his head and kisses me again. I release a groan that doesn't sound at all like me. It just feels so damn good.

He keeps kissing me as he sits down on the bed, me in his lap. He keeps kissing me as he pins me beneath him. I've been in his bedroom before, but never in his bed; it feels like a whole different world here.

When he slips his fingers into my shorts, I stiffen, but I immediately cover his hand with mine—I don't want him to pull back.

"I haven't had sex in over nine years," I say. "I'm a little out of practice."

"We can do whatever you like. I do have condoms, if you—"

"Have you been with anyone since we got married?" The words come out in a rush. Suddenly, it's imperative I know.

"No."

He shifts his hand lower, under my panties, and brushes a finger over my pussy. I moan. Then he withdraws, but it's only to remove the rest of my clothing; his hands are back between my legs a moment later.

Despite my desperation, being exposed makes me feel a bit nervous. It's been years since anyone saw me like this, and sex has always been complicated for me.

"Hey," he murmurs, his lips next to my ear. "You're gorgeous." He shifts down my body and licks my clit, oh-so-gently, but it's enough to nearly make me shoot off the bed.

He lifts his head and smiles. While the sight of Evan smiling isn't unfamiliar, this particular smile is different from anything I've seen before.

It has an edge of wickedness.

He dips his head again and licks near my clit without touching it directly. I don't recall being so sensitive before—is it because I haven't been with anyone in such a long time?

But before I can ponder that further, he slips one finger inside me and continues to lick me. I lose my ability to think straight as I grip the sheets and press myself against his face. One of his hands trails upward to my breasts, and he lazily pinches my nipple. It's overwhelming.

"Evan, can you..."

I don't even know what I'm asking for, but somehow, he knows. His tongue moves over my clit just right, and I come against him, a stream of nonsense escaping my mouth.

He crawls up my body and smiles down at me, my moisture clinging to his lips. I want to make him feel good, too, but as I reach for the waistband of his shorts and the high of the orgasm starts to fade, I feel a prickle of unease.

What if it's uncomfortable for me? It's been a long time, after all. Even if we don't have penetrative sex, I have a sensitive gag reflex, and I also remember getting a stiff jaw from blowjobs in the past.

Fortunately, from what I've been able to feel so far, he's not as big as my ex.

He rises up on his knees, and I pull his shorts and briefs down together. As I toss them off the bed, I examine his semi-hard cock.

Perfect.

He's slightly smaller than average—I believe—and this seems totally manageable. When I grin up at him, he dips his head to claim my mouth again. I stroke him as we kiss. His kisses become sloppier and inelegant, which is immensely satisfying. It appears I sort of know what I'm doing after all.

I lower my head, holding his gaze as I take his cock into my mouth and swirl my tongue around the tip. He hisses out a breath and sinks his hand into my hair. When he pulls, it stings a little, and I shake my head.

"Sorry," he says, lightening his touch.

"That's okay," I mumble, but he probably can't tell what I'm saying because I've still got him in my mouth. He's fully erect now, and it's the thought that I'm bringing him pleasure, more than anything else, that spurs me on.

But I'm starting to feel a strange emptiness between my legs, and eventually, I lift my head. "Where are those condoms?"

He removes a box from his bedside table, along with some lube. I can see that he's got some sex toys as well, but I don't get a good look before he closes the drawer and starts to roll on the condom. I settle onto my back, my pulse beating rapidly. Once he's sheathed himself, he bends down to kiss me, and I buck my hips against him, my breath shuddering as my pussy makes contact with the underside of his cock.

He slides his hand between our bodies and notches himself at my entrance, pushing inside slowly while keeping his gaze on my face.

"Okay?" he asks.

I nod enthusiastically.

He moves inside me with languid rolls of his hips. I bend my knees so he goes a little deeper, and I hold him tightly against me. I love being so close to him. The thought that he's inside me...it's enough to make my inner muscles squeeze, and he releases a guttural sound. He lifts his head, his hand fondly stroking my cheek.

I roll us over so I'm on top. The movement isn't as smooth as I'd like, but it gets the job done. It's okay that I'm not some sex goddess; he just wants to be with *me*.

I press sloppy kisses up and down his neck, and when he jerks his hips suddenly, I accidentally bite him.

"Shit!" I say. "I'm sorry."

"Don't apologize." He rubs my back. "I like it."

I still. "What, exactly, do you like?"

"Not a lot of pain, but...the edge of it."

I shift my mouth to his nipple. He groans and shoves a hand through his hair. My hand joins his, and I tug lightly as I start to thrust my hips again. We move in unison, our pace increasing. I can tell he's getting close, and I'm desperate for it. Desperate to make him feel as good as I can.

"I...*ahhh*." He holds me tightly as he comes inside me, and I bask in his pleasure.

After Evan disposes of the condom, I use the washroom. Then I return to his bed and slide on my underwear. He's put on his briefs but nothing else.

"Hey." He has another look on his face that I've never seen before. I suppose it's a content *I-just-had-an-orgasm* look, and I love that I'm responsible for it.

He pulls me against him, and we snuggle in silence for a few minutes. While cuddling is nothing new for us, cuddling while we're in bed and mostly naked—after having sex—is certainly different.

I had sex with my husband.

What does this mean? Where do we go from here?

I have lots of questions, but they don't seem pressing at the moment. I roll Evan onto his side so I'm behind him and he's the little spoon.

"Do you want me to sleep here?" I ask.

"Yes," he says. "Unless you want—"

"I want to stay."

I can't see it, but I know he's smiling.

Chapter 16

Evan

WHEN MY ALARM GOES off at seven, I'm momentarily disoriented. I'm in the same bed as usual, but there's someone else in my bed, which is certainly *not* usual.

Jane makes a muffled sound and throws her arm over my chest.

"Do you want to work out this morning?" I ask.

"No." Her voice is still heavy with sleep.

I hope she slept well last night. I did—much better than the night before, that's for sure. But as my brain slowly comes back online and she presses herself against my side, I don't feel quite so restful.

Did she simply want to do it once and get it out of her system? That doesn't sound like Jane, but what do I know?

When she kisses my shoulder, my worries start to snowball. I sit up, rub a hand over my eyes, and put on my glasses. The sheet barely covers her chest. If I push it down an inch or two, I'll be able to see her nipples, and while that's appealing, the idea of doing more than that...

Jane sits up next to me and frowns. "Is something wrong? Do you regret it?"

Shit.

"Definitely not," I say. "I'd been thinking about it for a while."

She lifts an eyebrow. "Since before we got married?"

"No. A few weeks, though it feels like longer. What about you?"

"Since Monday. I'm not used to wanting someone like this, and I couldn't deal with it. It was hugely distracting."

I chuckle and consider how to express what I'm feeling.

"The fact that I'm not jumping you now," I say slowly. "It doesn't mean that I don't want you, or that I don't hope we do it again, or that you're not beautiful first thing in the morning…" I pinch my brow. This is awkward, but I feel the need to be clear.

"Of course," she says. "I mean, I'm not so sure about the beautiful-first-thing-in-the-morning business, but everything else…of course."

"It's just…in my experience…right after you start having sex…there is the desire…to do it over and over again." To feel insatiable. "And that isn't me, not anymore."

"'Not anymore'?"

I scrub a hand over my face. "The antidepressants lower my libido. Occasionally, they also make it harder to get an erection."

"This was a problem in your last relationship?" she correctly surmises.

"Yeah."

She nods. "Don't worry, I'm not constantly horny. I was for the last three days, but now that we've done it…"

"You'll want to do it again, I hope?"

"Yeah, but probably not today."

I turn onto my side, pulling her against me. "Can we stay here for a little while?"

In response, she burrows against my chest. Mostly naked, but not as a prelude to anything. It's nice to know that this is enough for now, and I haven't disappointed her by not being up for more sex.

People don't always say what they mean, but I believe she was telling the truth—and it's not because she identifies as demisexual. She rarely feels attraction, but that doesn't mean she can't have a high libido, and it doesn't say anything about how much she wants sex when she does feel attraction.

She runs her fingers over my neck.

"Is there a mark?" I ask.

"Maybe a faint one?" She tilts her head. "Or not. Hard to tell without the lights on." Morning sunlight filters through the curtains, however, and I can see her reasonably well, even if she has trouble assessing a bite mark. "What else do you like?"

"Hm?"

"I mean, in bed. So I know. For next time."

I'm glad to hear her talk about *next time*.

"I like and have done...lots of different things," I say.

"You seemed to like when I bit you and pulled your hair."

"Yes." I pause. "I like being spanked, too."

"I'll keep that in mind."

I exhale unsteadily, but it's not as if I want her to spank me now, even if I look forward to it in the future. "And you?"

"I don't like anything too rough, and I can rarely orgasm more than once, so don't feel the need to try for multiple orgasms."

A week ago, I wouldn't have imagined I'd be in bed with Jane, talking about sex. But neither of us has spoken about what this means—and what it changes in our marriage.

While Jane's in the shower, I get dressed and head downstairs. I start the coffeemaker, then debate what to do with Watson. I feel like he should have a special outfit today, but what? He's already decked out in Mardi Gras beads, and in the past few weeks, I've gone through a good number of my accessories.

When I hear the water stop, I knock Watson to the ground, facedown, and set Mr. Frog on top of him. Then I head outside with our mugs of coffee.

A few minutes later, Jane steps outside in a camisole and shorts.

"What happened?" She nods toward the living room.

I shrug. "He had a busy night."

She laughs, and I can't help the joy that brings me. Yes, after sex and a good night's sleep and a good morning after, I'm more relaxed than I've felt in a while.

"Any particular plans for the day?" I ask.

The sort of thing I might normally say. In some ways, this morning feels like all the others in our short marriage...but not quite. I reach for her free hand—the one that's not holding her mug—and squeeze. Again, something I might have done just a few days ago.

"The usual," she replies.

"Sounds good to me."

We work in our separate offices, two floors apart. We eat lunch together. At the end of the workday, I go for my usual walk and come back extra sweaty because it's disgustingly humid.

For dinner, we have leftovers, and for dessert, we finish the egg tarts. Once again, a crumb clings to her bottom lip, and this time, I feel free to lean forward and wipe it off. She licks the crumb off my finger.

"Can you watch an episode without jumping me today?" I ask with faux sternness.

"I think I can manage," she says.

She cuddles up against me, and at one particularly romantic moment, she does kiss me—but without the urgency of the last two nights. We have to rewind the show, but only a minute or two.

I like these kisses, too. I hope they continue to be part of our marriage.

At the end of the evening, we stand in the upstairs hallway together, and she gives me a hug goodnight. As she steps back, the idea that she might sleep in a bed that isn't mine...it makes me feel hollow.

"Would you like to sleep in my bed?" I ask. "Not for sex. Just because I want to have you there, but if you'd rather sleep alone—"

She cuts me off by placing a finger to my lips, then walks into my bedroom while my feet are still rooted to the floor. I admire her ass in those little shorts she wears to sleep, and unlike that time she was mowing the grass, I don't feel guilty about it.

She settles under the covers on what is, I guess, her side of the bed, and puts her phone on the bedside table that I never use. I pull her against me and kiss her neck. When I shift back, I smile at her and brush the hair away from her face.

Like yesterday, she falls asleep quickly, but I don't, much as I like having her here. I still have doubts about our sexual compatibility, given that it caused such problems in my last relationship. It's natural for there to be differences in how often two people want sex—and what kind of sex they want. A little compromise isn't an issue for me, but I still worry. What if it's more than a little?

We can't just "break up." I mean, we can, but there's a lot to lose. We made a commitment: we're married and we own a house together.

Have we complicated everything?

And how, exactly, does she feel? Is her sexual interest in me a sign that her feelings are much deeper than before? I suspect it is—I know that's how it worked for her in the past—and the idea delights me.

But maybe it's different this time.

I fear I won't be able to sleep, but eventually, the sound of Jane's rhythmic breathing pulls me under.

Chapter 17

Jane

"So, you did it?" Claudia asks. "Was it satisfactory?"

I blush. "More the satisfactory. Better than it's ever been for me before, to be honest."

I haven't slept in my bed for the past two nights, but I'm using it for a video call with Claudia while Evan is on his usual walk. Then I'll go downstairs and cook dinner.

"Don't worry, I'll spare you the details," I say. "Actually, if you want me to stop talking about this completely…"

"No, no, it's okay. I get that it's the biggest thing happening in your life right now, and I want to know. It's not like you're trying to convince me that *I* should get married and have sex, and that if I find the right person, 'everything will change.'"

"Oh God, no."

"I know, so it's all good."

People have wanted to change me, too. The friend who made me feel like a bad feminist, for example. I rarely spoke about the fact that I hadn't had sex in years, but I know some people would have felt it was a problem that needed to be fixed ASAP.

Evan was actually the first person who suggested I could be on the ace spectrum. I'd thought it didn't apply to me because I do have a libido, and I had—twice, at that point—been sexually attracted to someone, but he suggested I do more research.

He wasn't wrong.

"My mother texted me earlier," Claudia says. "Her friend's daughter found someone on a dating app, and they're getting married. She wants me to try using the app. Actually, she's already made me a profile."

"Noooo," I say.

"I keep explaining that I'm aroace and while it's not the same for everyone, I'm uninterested in dating and marriage. But she refuses to accept it."

The first time Claudia complained about her mother to me, she immediately felt guilty, knowing mine is gone, but I insisted it was fine. If hers was trying to get her to do something that she'd asserted—over and over again—she didn't want, she was free to complain.

They don't have a close relationship. Sometimes they go months without talking, like me and my father. But my father never tries to interfere in my life.

I've also never told him that I'm demisexual. I suspect he'd wonder why I was telling him, then frown and say, "Isn't that normal? At least for a woman?"

I talk to Claudia for a little longer, and then I find myself looking at my wedding pictures. It's the first time I've done it since Evan and I slept together. When I get to the picture of us kissing, I stare at it for a long time, and I imagine telling my former self about what would end up happening. A burst of laughter escapes my lips.

Come to think of it, I've been laughing more these days.

"This weekend," Evan says as we eat dinner, "Isobel and Daisy invited us over. Do you want to come, or would you prefer I go without you?"

"I'll go with you."

He smiles at me, and for some reason, I find it devastating. And when he touches my leg under the table...

How do I tell him that I'm interested in having sex tonight, if he is? I could, of course, straddle him while we're watching TV again, but I'd prefer not to do that every time.

I'm not very experienced at this sort of thing.

"Is something wrong?" he asks.

Sometimes, I wish he wasn't so aware of every little change in my body language—he's become even more attuned to me lately.

But I sort of love that about him, too.

Not that I *love* love him, in the way many people love their spouses, but I'm extremely fond of him.

"Do you want to have sex after we clean up?" I say in a rush. It feels neither romantic nor sexy, but it gets the point across.

In response, he smiles again, and my skin prickles as he slides his hand even farther up my leg.

After cutting the grass on Saturday afternoon, I take a shower and put on proper clothes for our dinner with Isobel and Daisy. Nothing too fancy: jeans and a black blouse that just came out of the wash.

"You look nice." Evan kisses me on the cheek as we put on our shoes by the front door.

I do feel pretty, but as he drives us toward his cousin's, I feel a strange itch on my shoulder. Hmm. Maybe it's because I'm in close proximity to Evan—this is the first time we've been in the car together since we started having sex. And since I started feeling attracted to him, which was less than a week ago.

Yeah, it probably has something to do with sexual attraction, and I'm just not used to it.

We arrive at the apartment building, which is in the north part of Toronto, and park in visitor parking. We're buzzed in and proceed to the fifth floor. I've got a bottle of wine in my left hand.

Isobel opens the door, and Nolan is right behind her.

"Uncle Evan!" Nolan flings himself at Evan's leg. "Do you want to see my new car?"

"Your new car?" Evan says. "I didn't know you were old enough to drive."

Nolan giggles. With a hand that looks a bit sticky, he grabs Evan's wrist.

"Do you remember who this is?" Isobel asks Nolan before he can scamper off. She gestures toward me.

I stand there awkwardly as Nolan looks me up and down. Under his scrutiny, I feel that itch under my shirt again.

He shakes his head. "Who are you?"

"I'm Jane." After handing the wine bottle to Isobel—who murmurs her thanks—I bend down, both to get closer to Nolan's height and to take off my shoes.

"Remember we went to a wedding earlier this summer?" Isobel says. "That was Uncle Evan and Auntie Jane's wedding."

Nolan twists his lips. "I remember," he says to me. "But you looked different then."

"Yes, I was wearing a white dress."

"Like a princess." He pauses and tilts his head. "You don't look like a princess now."

I shouldn't be insulted that a four-year-old is telling me I don't look like a princess, yet I feel a smidgen of irrational disappointment.

"I think she looks very pretty," Evan says as I stand up. He puts a hand on my lower back, which, weirdly enough, has started to itch.

"She is pretty." Nolan nods solemnly. "But she doesn't look like a princess."

"What do I look like?" I ask. "A stegosaurus?"

I hope I'm doing okay at this. I haven't spent much time around children. Even when my half-siblings were this age—and that was over a decade ago—I didn't see them often. Yet despite my lack of experience, I want to have kids of my own.

"No!" He laughs. "Stegosauruses don't wear jeans."

Well, then. That sounds pretty definitive.

Nolan proudly shows us his Hot Wheels and spends ten minutes lining up the cars while making loud zoom noises. When he and Evan are busy adjusting the track, I itch my back before taking a sip of wine and helping myself to some baby carrots.

Isobel's wife, Daisy, announces that dinner is ready a few minutes later, and we crowd around the table and eat spaghetti and meatballs and the most delicious garlic bread I've ever had. When I ask Daisy for the recipe, I feel extremely domestic. But my skin is still itchy, and even homemade pie isn't enough to make me forget about it.

Once dinner is finished, Nolan wants to play at the park. After making sure he's gone to the washroom so he—hopefully—doesn't have to go while he's out, Isobel asks if Evan and I would mind taking him by ourselves. Evan looks at me, and when I don't have any objections, he nods.

Nolan assures us that he knows the way and we "don't have to look at our phones" to get there. As we take the elevator, I think about how different the world is from the one I grew up in, how different our children's childhood would be from our own.

When we have to cross the "big street," Nolan reaches for Evan's hand without being asked, and for some reason, that makes my eyes water. If I saw a random person holding a kid's hand, it wouldn't affect me, but the fact that it's Evan—and a child whom I'll watch grow up, presuming I don't fuck up this marriage...

"Look at me, Auntie Jane!" Nolan calls, rushing up a slide. A smaller child watches avidly, perhaps trying to figure out whether she, too, can use slides in that way.

But it's those words, so easily spoken, that stop me in my tracks. Sure, his mother introduced me as that, but now he's calling me "auntie" without any prompting.

"Oh wow!" I say, unable to come up with any more words.

Evan also looks toward me, and something catches in my throat. How did I not realize before that he's incredibly good-looking? I know this is how things work for me, but it seems impossible now, given how much I'm affected by him. There's something about him that just makes me...itch.

At the top of the slide, Nolan turns around. He's about to slide back down when the smaller child puts her foot onto the slide and tries to climb. An adult whisks her away just as Nolan releases his grasp on the edge of the slide.

"Did you see me?" He runs up to me.

"I did. Is that one of yours?" I point to a toy car on the ground near the slide.

"Benny!" he cries, running toward it. He grabs the car and runs back to me.

"How many other cars do you have in your pockets?" I ask.

He holds out two.

"Do you want me to keep them safe while you play?"

He nods vigorously, hands them over, and goes back to the playground, this time deciding to tackle the swings while I sit on the bench. He can get himself moving a little, but not too well, and he asks Evan to give him pushes so he can go higher.

It's a nice way to spend an evening, something as simple as going to the playground. I have vague memories of going to the park with both of my parents, the memories pleasant but tinged with sadness because of everything that came afterward. I absently rub my hand over Benny's wheels.

Hm. My lower back is getting itchy again. I set the cars in my lap and discreetly reach behind me to scratch my back, over top of my shirt.

There. That feels a bit better.

"Did a dog lick you?" Nolan asks.

Where did he come from? How is he suddenly in front of me?

So much for being discreet.

At my puzzled look, he says, "One time, a puppy licked me, and I got itchy. Mommy says I probably have an allergy."

Everything suddenly slots into place. The weird things happening to my body? I've been blaming them all on the unfamiliar feeling of attraction, but this is definitely something else.

As Nolan begins talking to a boy about his age, Evan sits on the bench beside me. I try to ignore the warmth radiating from him.

"This is nice," he says, echoing my earlier thoughts.

"Uh. Yeah. Evan?"

"Hm?"

We both have our gazes on Nolan, who is now racing the other kid.

"When you did the laundry," I say, "what kind of detergent did you use?"

"They were out of the usual one at the grocery store, so I got what was on sale."

I was right. This hasn't happened in over a decade, which is why I didn't immediately realize what was going on.

"I told you," I say, "to always buy the same detergent. This one gives me contact dermatitis." To emphasize this, I scratch myself again, but then I stiffen.

Are we going to have a fight in the middle of a public park?

Maybe I should have kept the annoyance out of my voice, but I couldn't seem to help it. I *told* him what to do, and he didn't listen...or ask if it was okay to buy something else.

My shoulders are hunched up near my shoulders as I watch Nolan on the playground. Maybe being with someone is too complicated. Being alone is simpler. And if we have kids, there will be even more conflict...

"Hey." Evan puts a hand on my knee. "I'm really sorry. This is my fault. Tomorrow, first thing, I'll buy the right one, no matter how many stores I have to go to, and rewash all your clothes. Actually, maybe I should wash the machine first to make sure there's no residue—does vinegar help? I'll look it up."

I just stare at him.

Why didn't I expect him to be understanding? Because I've seen Suzanne and my father have long arguments over the stupidest shit? They don't argue a lot, but when they do, it's bad.

And my last relationship was so long ago, and we never lived together...and it's easy to imagine that my ex would have refused to believe I could be so sensitive to detergent, at least by the end.

But this is Evan. Of course he would trust me to know what's happening to my body, and he's able to admit he screwed up.

"Hey," he says again. "I know you're spiraling—I do that too sometimes, like when the air conditioning stopped working. I don't know why it's happening to you now, but I'm so sorry.

I'm not sure why it didn't occur to me that you had a really good reason for always using the same detergent—"

"I should have told you the reason."

"No, no. You said to always get the same one, and I was thoughtless. I swear I'll fix it as soon as I can. Do you want to go home now?"

I squeeze the toy cars in my lap. "Not right away, but I don't want to stay late." I scratch my waist, and Evan looks pained for a moment, like my distress hurts him.

But he papers that over a moment later, as if afraid I'll try to assure him that I'm okay, and he doesn't want me to try to soothe him.

God, relationships are complicated.

"At first," I say, "I thought the itching was, like, a strange expression of physical attraction. Since, you know, I'm not used to experiencing attraction."

He looks like he's trying to hold back laughter, but when I chuckle, he chuckles, too.

Marriage isn't quite what I thought it would be.

"Where's Benny?" Nolan is right in front of me again, and I'm disoriented for a moment, but I manage to hold up the correct car.

"Are you ready to go home?" Evan asks.

"No!"

"Five more minutes, okay?"

"Okay, but Auntie Jane has to come with me." He grabs my hand and takes me toward the swings. He rarely seems to walk anywhere; he's always running. "Sit down," he commands, pointing to a swing.

I sit. He tries to push me, but I don't move much. When he pushes me again, giggling, I make myself swing, just a little.

"Here, let me help you," Evan says.

He moves behind me, and now there are two pairs of hands on my back, one much larger than the other. Evan's hands are higher, and they push me gently but firmly, and I don't have to make myself swing this time. Nolan's giggles ease something jagged inside me.

"Okay," Evan says at last. "It's been five minutes—"

"How do you know?" Nolan asks. "You didn't look at your phone."

Eventually, Evan manages to coax Nolan away from the playground, and we head back to the apartment building. There's a bit of a slowdown when Nolan wants to eat some so-called blueberries off a bush—they're definitely not blueberries—but we get there eventually.

As dusk starts to settle, Evan drives us home. I'd planned to drive back, but he said I should have my hands free to scratch myself. How sexy.

At home, I remove the offending articles of clothing, take an antihistamine, have a shower, and put on some clothes that I know weren't washed in the last load. I give my shirt a sniff. The difference in scent is very faint, which must be why I didn't notice earlier.

When Evan walks around his bedroom while brushing his teeth, I'm already in his bed, and he looks a little surprised to see me here.

"Do you want me to sleep in my room today?" I feel a flicker of disappointment, but he's free to have his bed to himself if he wants.

"No, I'm glad you're here. I just thought you might not want..."

"Of course I want."

He smiles at me as well as he can with a toothbrush in his mouth, then returns to the bathroom, and I think back on what I said.

Of course.

But I only started sharing his bed less than a week ago. It was never the plan, yet now it seems only right.

When he climbs in next to me, I pull him close.

"Let's go out tomorrow night," I murmur.

Chapter 18

Evan

I WAKE UP JUST after seven on Sunday morning. My most important task for the day: to buy new detergent and rewash Jane's clothes.

I can't believe I didn't at least check with her when I bought different detergent. I feel like a clueless, incompetent husband, and I never want to be one of those.

Yeah, you're an idiot.

I try to shut up that voice in my head. Everyone makes mistakes sometimes. It's fine. But I hate that I made Jane uncomfortable and she started freaking out.

I'm oddly touched that she lets herself freak out in front of me now. She doesn't normally do that with her friends, and I'm sure she doesn't do it with her family.

I still want to give her father a piece of my mind. It's rare for me to feel anger toward someone—and I've never even met him. Usually, my anger is directed inward. But he didn't show up to his daughter's wedding. The bar is so low. I think I may have apologized more for doing laundry incorrectly than he apologized for missing the wedding.

I'm filled with restless energy. I feel the need to do something with it, but as I sit up, Jane pulls me back down. I roll over to face her. She has a little sleep in her eyes and her hair is mussed—I think she looks lovely.

"Morning," she mumbles.

I'm overwhelmed by feelings that I don't want to think about too much. I'm afraid to put them into words. She strokes her hand down my side, and I start to get hard.

"Not itchy this morning?" I ask.

"Nope."

When she puts her hand on my inner thigh, I spring into action. I don't need to take off my glasses because I didn't even have a chance to put them on. I lean forward and kiss her; her body molds itself against mine.

For a split second, I feel like I'm watching this unfold from a distance. Because it's difficult to believe this is actually happening to *me*. How did I get so lucky?

She flips us over, and once she's seated on top of me, she whips her shirt over her head, and I cup her breasts. She dips her head to claim my mouth, then shifts her lips to my neck, moving down to my nipple next. She takes it into her mouth and nibbles lightly.

"Do you like that?" she asks.

"Yes," I groan.

She does it to the other nipple, then reaches between my legs and strokes behind my balls; I arch against her. She keeps moving down my body, licking a trail to my bellybutton; my skin feels cooler in the wake of her tongue. All my attention is focused on where she's touching me—and where she just touched.

I slide my hand through her hair, careful not to tug because I know she doesn't like that. She, however, scrapes her fingernails down my lower back, then lifts my hips toward her mouth as she takes my cock between her lips.

In an instant, I'm completely hard.

Jane sucks me nearly to the base before releasing me with a *pop*. She gives me a few tugs and laps up my precum. I groan both at the sensation as well as the image of her bent over me, her tongue peeking out from between her lips. She's gorgeous. Her brows are drawn together, as though she's concentrating very hard on her task.

Needing to touch her, I sit up. She releases me again, and I turn her onto her back and slip my fingers between her legs. She's incredibly wet for me, and I add to her wetness by giving her a long, slow lick. I make sure I'm not too forceful on her clit; she doesn't like that. I curve one finger toward me as I lick her gently. She makes a sound I can't describe in the back of her throat, and I can feel her flex her legs. She doesn't allow many people to see her like this, and I can't help feeling special.

Spurred on by her soft sounds, I pick up my pace, and she grips the sheets. I glance up at her pretty parted lips and move my hand in the way she seems to like the best. She comes undone, clenching around my finger.

Afterward, she lies limp in bed, and for a moment, I wonder if this is it for her. If so, that's okay. I can get myself off, and it won't take long. But then she pushes me onto my stomach and lies on top of me. She rolls her hips against mine, pressing me against the bed, and it feels so good to be underneath her like this. She reaches for my cock and starts jerking me off, and I lift my hips to give her better access. Her other hand moves to my ass. She gives me a light smack.

"Harder?" she asks.

"Yes," I say. "Please."

Her next smack is a little harder, enough to make it sting for a few seconds. The sort of sting that can make you forget, however briefly, about everything—especially when your wife is jacking you off at the same time. I thrust against her hand, against the mattress, not really thinking about what I'm doing, just needing to move. She spanks me again, and I swear I'm about to lose my mind. She leans forward and nibbles on my earlobe, the slightest brush of teeth against my skin. Pulling my hair, she turns my head to the side, and my lips immediately find hers. We kiss urgently. I want to live in this moment forever, but I also want to...

"I'm almost..." I begin.

I'm not sure if I expect her to turn me over so I don't make a mess of the bed, but she doesn't, and I'm beyond caring. How can I? All that matters is her touch, her quickening pace on my cock.

She slaps my ass one more time and...*God*. I jerk against her hand and come on the sheets with a satisfied growl, pouring out everything I can't put into words.

Gentler now, she rolls me onto my back and lies next to me.

"Was that good?" she asks.

I laugh because it seems like such a ridiculous question, and I'm sometimes giggly after an orgasm anyway. But perhaps she really is unsure. "It was great. Luckily, I was planning to do laundry today."

She chuckles. "I was trying to...the way you said..."

My brain isn't working well right now, but I kiss her cheek reassuringly. I'm not unaccustomed to a partner wanting to make me feel good, yet something about her earnestness and shyness and vulnerability makes my chest squeeze. Makes this feel a little different. We lie there in post-orgasmic bliss for a while.

"Just so know," I say, "I have no intention of sleeping with anyone else, now that we've..." I gesture between us. "And yes, I'm sure." I'm unable to explain exactly what I feel, but I know that much is true. I only want her.

She responds with a kiss and jumps in the shower. I strip the bed before making coffee.

When she comes downstairs and sees Watson wearing my apron, she laughs, but when she looks at me over her mug and smiles, I know she's thinking of what we did earlier.

Jane's laundry is redone and folded by early afternoon, and I hope I've made it clear that it's a mistake I'll never make again. Though I do errantly think that if she couldn't wear clothes, it wouldn't be such a bad thing.

I do more chores after lunch, then we watch TV before getting ready for our night out.

"Do you want me to do your makeup again?" she asks as we reach the top of the stairs, about to head to our separate bedrooms.

"If you'd like to," I say.

She nods. "It's kinda fun to do stuff I'm not interested in wearing myself."

I put on a silk shirt and knock on her door. It feels like the right thing to do even if I saw her naked this morning.

"Come in," she says.

Jane is wearing dark jeans, paired with a cream-colored sleeveless shirt, a contrast to the black clothes she usually favors for going out. When she beckons me in and turns around, I see that the shirt is mostly backless, aside from a big bow just above her ass.

God, she's gorgeous.

"Is it too much?" she asks, worrying her red lip.

"Definitely not. It looks great." I mime undoing the bow, which earns me a fond eye roll.

She follows me to the en suite. "Tell me what you want."

I gesture to the makeup and show her a few pictures on my phone. She immediately gets to work. She starts with the pink and blue eyeshadow before moving to the eyeliner. I focus on her slightly parted lips and intent gaze as she glams me up.

"Do you like it?" she asks. "I think it's pretty."

I'm not sure how she knew *that* was the word I wanted to hear today, but it is.

"I love it," I tell her, just like I did last time.

But this time, I press a kiss to her cheek afterward.

It takes a long time to get to downtown Toronto, and when we finally arrive at the queer-owned Italian restaurant on Queen West, we're almost ten minutes late. We're immediately shown to our table on the small back patio, which I requested when I made the reservation.

"Evan!" says Lyla, our server, as she pours our water. "You haven't been here in ages."

"I got married and moved to Richmond Hill."

It's nice to be back downtown—I've missed it. But I don't feel the need to come here all the time. I like our house with its backyard.

"Congratulations," she says. "You look great."

"Thanks. This is my wife, Jane."

Lyla tells us about the daily specials, but since I don't eat here often anymore, I decide to go with my usual: linguine with clams. Jane selects the calamari, at my recommendation, as well as a glass of wine, and we choose the carpaccio to start. There have been some small changes to the menu in the past year, but all the things I like best are still available.

Yet as we wait for our food, I think of the fact that I've been on dates here before. It feels wrong that this isn't a special place just for me and Jane.

"What's wrong?" she asks.

"Just thinking about the dates I've taken to this restaurant." I grimace. "Sorry."

"No, it's fine. I know you dated other people before we got married."

"Still, it feels weird." I chuckle awkwardly. "And weirder to bring it up."

She shrugs. "I want to go to the places you like. Actually..." She looks around. "I'm pretty sure you took me here once before. A long time ago, before the pandemic. In winter, maybe? It wasn't nice enough to sit on the patio."

A vague memory comes to mind. "With Lana and Camila?"

"Yeah. When they first started dating but weren't ready to tell anyone, so they pretended nothing was happening."

"And we spoke afterward and agreed something was *definitely* happening?"

"They were holding hands under the table," Jane says.

I place my hand on her knee. She puts her hand on top of mine, and we smile dopily at each other.

What is this?

Well, it's pretty clear that I'm falling in love with someone, yet again. That's the problem with me: I've fallen in love many times, with many different kinds of people, and it's never worked out.

But I think of her touching up my eyeshadow, pulling my hair as she lies on top of me and jerks me off...and I wonder how I can help it. I didn't expect this to happen. I'd known Jane for a long time; I thought I knew what our marriage would be like. But somehow, everything has changed.

The real problem is that now, there's so much more to lose, yet that doesn't mean this time will be different.

In most of my relationships, I was the one who was dumped. Someone found me lacking. What will she find lacking about me?

Or maybe she's not falling for me the way I'm falling for her. I don't think that's true, after everything that has happened between us now, but I've been wrong before. And if I'm wrong and I say something, it will be more than a little awkward.

Fortunately, our food starts arriving, and I try to focus on the taste and smells, losing myself in the sensory experience so I can stop myself from spiraling. When Jane heads to the washroom before dessert, I stare at the bow on the back of her shirt and imagine undoing it.

And many hours later—after we walk around downtown at night and head back to Richmond Hill—I untie that bow, and the shirt falls to the floor in my room.

The next day is a holiday Monday. Jane decides she still wants to work out. When I come downstairs to start the coffee, I notice Watson has stolen the shirt that I wore last night, and I laugh.

And when Jane joins me for coffee outside, I point to Watson and ask what he's doing.

"Why would I have any idea?" she asks.

The way she says it, with a completely straight face, not even a hint of a smile...yeah, I'm in deep trouble.

Chapter 19

Jane

On Thursday afternoon, I'm hard at work (sort of) in my home office when the doorbell rings. The last person who rang our doorbell wanted to convert us to their religion, but since it could be the package I'm expecting, I head downstairs. However, when I open the door, it's clear this isn't a delivery.

There's a woman and a little girl on the doorstep. Our next-door neighbors. I've seen them from a distance, but I've never talked to them before. The dark-haired girl is wearing a *Frozen* knapsack, her hands gripping the purple straps.

"Hi," the woman says. "Is Evan here?"

"Sorry, he's not," I say.

"I thought he worked from home?"

"Usually, but not this afternoon." He has a rare in-person meeting.

The woman hesitates. She has a panicked look on her face, but I have no idea what's going on. "I'm Deena. I know we've never spoken before, but our husbands are friends, and I was hoping he—or you?—could do me a favor. My father had a heart attack, and he's at the hospital, and I'd prefer not to bring Skylar. Could you watch her? Just for an hour, until Gordon gets home."

"Of course."

"Thank you so much..."

"Jane. I'm Jane."

Deena bends down and puts her hands on her daughter's shoulders. "Be good for Jane, okay? Here's the key to our house if you need it."

She hurries down the driveway before I can say anything, and I recall the last time I went to the hospital—when I was about Skylar's age. Fortunately, I haven't needed to go since my mom died.

I'm surprised that Deena left Skylar with me, given she doesn't know me at all, but I understand not wanting to bring a child to a hospital in an emergency, and I guess she knows Evan. Besides, people are probably more comfortable leaving kids with an unfamiliar woman than an unfamiliar man.

I curse myself for not making an effort to get to know our neighbors. When I lived in a high-rise, I didn't know my neighbors, either, but now that we have a house, it feels different.

I look down at Skylar, who's still gripping the straps of her knapsack. I'd usually do another hour of work, but it's not like I have anything critical that needs to get done today.

"Would you feel more comfortable at your house?" I ask, making my voice slightly more upbeat than usual.

She nods, looking down.

Once I put on my shoes and grab everything I need, we head next door. Skylar struggles with the key in the lock, so I do it for her.

The layout of the house is a little different from ours, but the biggest difference is that it's clearly home to a kid, as evidenced by all the colorful toys.

"Can I have a snack?" Skylar asks. "I haven't had one yet."

"Sure." I follow her into the kitchen. "What do you usually eat?"

"Ants on a log. I can make it myself."

I watch as she pulls a Tupperware of cut celery out of the fridge, followed by a jar of peanut butter. Then she grabs a butter knife and a plate.

"Can you get the raisins for me? Please?" She points to a high cupboard.

It's rare for me to help someone reach something—I'm not exactly tall—so this is a nice change. I get the bag of raisins, and she gets to work on making her snack at the kitchen table.

I haven't looked after a kid by myself in years. I find myself wishing that Evan were here, but this seems manageable. She's fairly independent; she just can't be left by herself.

Though I've never had ants on a log before, I have a sneaking suspicion that they don't usually involve this much peanut butter or this many raisins.

"You can have some." Skylar gestures to the food laid out on the table.

I shake my head. "Maybe later."

We sit there in silence for a couple of minutes while she munches on her celery. I feel like I should say something, but I'm not sure what.

"School just started, right?" I say. "What grade are you in?"

She holds up a single finger, then pushes around the food on her plate. "Will my zaidy be okay?"

Oh dear.

"Um. I don't know." I have no idea what the situation is, and I have distinct memories of being told my mother was going to be okay—and she wasn't. I don't wish to lie to this child I barely know. "I hope so." I pause. "My friend's grandfather had a heart attack, and he lived for a long time afterward."

This is true. Lana's grandfather had a heart attack when we were in university, and he just passed away last year. But I don't know much about this sort of thing—or how to talk to children about it.

"Maybe you could make him a card?" I say. "A get-well-soon card?"

Skylar nods as she crunches her celery.

When she finishes her snack, she brings her dishes to the sink and puts the celery and peanut butter away, then wipes a hand on her shirt as she heads to the next room.

"Skylar," I say, "how about you wash your hands before you make the card?" I fear that if she doesn't, the paper will be covered in peanut butter.

She scurries to the washroom and returns a minute later. As she folds a piece of paper in half and gets to work, I sit on the couch and text Evan to tell him where I am. I don't want him to worry when he returns to an empty house. He doesn't immediately respond, but I don't expect him to—I assume he's either on the road or still in his meeting.

"How do you spell 'get well soon'?" Skylar asks.

I tell her, and she writes each letter down on the front of the card.

Even though she looks nothing like I did at that age, I can't help seeing my younger self in her. It seems horribly unfair that a young child could lose a parent—or even a grandparent—but I was in grade one when my mom passed away.

I scroll through social media on my phone, not really seeing the words or the pictures, just needing to do something with my hands.

"Is this okay?" Skylar sits down beside me. On the front of her card, there are two people and a rainbow, plus something else that might be a dog. Inside, she's written, "I love you. Skylar."

"It's very nice," I tell her, swallowing. No one has said—or written—those three little words to me in over twenty years. Though I've said them myself, they haven't been returned.

She scampers off. I poke my head out of the doorway to see where she's going. She puts the card on the bench by the door before returning. She pulls a tablet out of her *Frozen* backpack, as well as some headphones, and starts watching an animated show that's unfamiliar to me. Since I haven't been given any instructions on screentime, I figure this is fine. I'm a last-minute babysitter in an emergency; I just have to make sure she's safe and fed.

My thoughts drift to wondering what my kids would be like. Does Evan still want kids? I assume so, but we haven't spoken about it recently.

When Skylar takes off her headphones, an hour has passed since she arrived on my doorstep. Her father still isn't home.

"What would you like to do now?" I ask.

"Can we go outside?"

"Sure. Just on the driveway or in the backyard."

At the front of the house, she tells me the code to the garage—she's too short to enter it herself, but she knows it. I open it up, and she reaches for a skipping rope. "You can skip, too." She gestures to another rope. "That one's longer. I got them for my birthday."

Since I don't need to spend more time on my phone, I pick up a rope and start skipping, something I haven't done since I was a child. Is jumping rope as popular as it used to be? We used to do it at recess. I cross my arms in front of me, then switch to skipping backward. Skylar watches me for a moment before she begins skipping herself.

"I'm not very good," she says.

"What? You're plenty good."

"But I can't do what you do."

Now I feel like I was trying to show off, but that wasn't my intention. "You just need a little practice. What do you want to do? Skip backward?"

She nods.

I don't know how to explain it; it's just something I remember how to do, like riding a bike. "Start with the rope in front of you. Now raise it up and behind."

She tries to copy me, but the rope hits her shoes. She tries one more time, without success. "I can't do it."

Should I encourage her to continue trying? It doesn't feel like this is outside of her abilities, and it's good to learn how to keep trying, even if it's not easy for you the first time.

But I've known this kid for an hour, and her grandfather is in the hospital.

I try to think of what my father was like with me at this age—his patience as he taught me to ride a bike—and there's a twinge of pain in my chest, but it quickly dissipates. It remains hard, however, to think of how close my dad and I used to be, and how the opposite is true now.

"Maybe you can try for a little longer," I say. "But if you can't do it, you can try again another day. Some things take time." I know the passing of time feels different when you're a kid, though.

After a few more minutes, I can tell she's getting frustrated. I encourage her to jump forward—she's pretty good at that—before she tries again. Build up some confidence.

And then...she does it. She stops after one, excited with her success.

"Jane! Did you see me?"

"I did! You were great."

Her face splits into a grin.

She tries again. The rope hits her feet, but she's buoyed by the fact that she did it once, and the next time, she does it twice in a row.

Then her gaze drifts to the left. Evan has driven up.

Chapter 20

Evan

As I GET OUT of the car, I hear Jane say, "My husband is home."

It stops me in my tracks.

It's the first time I've heard her refer to me like that, and the words fall so easily—so naturally—from her lips. I like how it sounds, and I can't help smiling.

Yes, that's me. Her husband.

Eventually, I manage to make myself move, and I head next door. I received her text, so I'm not surprised she's outside with Skylar.

"Hi, Evan," Skylar says. "Look what I can do." She skips backward a few times, and as I watch her, I also watch Jane out of the corner of my eye. She looks pleased...and proud.

"Wow," I say.

"Jane taught me. Can you do it?"

Jane hands her rope to me, and when her fingers brush mine, I feel a prickle of awareness. It puts me off-balance, and perhaps that's why the rope hits my shoes when I try to skip backward. Or maybe it's because I haven't done this in many, many years.

I succeed on my next attempt, and I do it a few times before stopping. These shoes are not made for such activity. As my wife take the rope from me, Gordon parks on the bottom half of the driveway.

"Daddy!" Skylar drops her rope and rushes toward him, and he lifts her up as he gets out of the car. "Is Zaidy okay? Is he out of the hospital? Can I go see him?"

"He'll probably be there for a few days, but maybe you can visit him after school tomorrow. We'll see how he's doing."

"I made him a card."

"Yeah? You can show me."

But first, she wants to show off her skipping skills.

"Thank you so much for looking after her," Gordon says to Jane. "Deena didn't want to bring her to the hospital in an emergency."

"No problem," she says. "We had a good time together. I'm glad I could help."

A wave of fondness washes over me. I know this situation might not have been the easiest for Jane, and it happened to coincide with when of the rare times I wasn't home during the day.

We speak for a few more minutes, and then I take my wife's hand and lead her into our house. She's a little sweaty, and her hair is tied up in a messy bun.

"How was it?" I ask.

"It was a bit awkward at first, and I didn't know how to answer her questions about her grandfather, but it went well."

"Do you have any work left to finish?"

She shakes her head. "It's fine. I'll do it tomorrow."

I go for my usual walk, then return home and have a shower. When I come downstairs, Jane is crouched on the floor by the back door.

"Now stay still," she murmurs—to Watson? "You can do it."

I chuckle and wonder if this is how she was encouraging Skylar.

The sound of my laughter draws her attention, and Jane whips her head toward me, looking slightly embarrassed that I've caught her speaking to a giant plushie.

"What's Watson doing?" I ask.

"Wearing a clip-on bowtie." She shifts to the side so I can see the red bowtie. Is that hers? I don't think I own one like that. "But it wasn't clipping well to his fluff."

"It looks good. Apparently, a chonky penguin can pull off a crooked bowtie."

She turns back to Watson and adjusts the bow so it's straight. I'm not sure why, but the fact that my rather serious wife is on the floor next to a large plush penguin, after skipping with the little girl next door...

I can't help sitting down next to Jane and planting a kiss on her mouth. She winds her arms around my back and returns the kiss, and I smile against her lips.

Jane climbs into my bed that night wearing a white T-shirt and navy shorts. There's something tantalizing about her loose clothes—and the fact that I know what's underneath. When she sets aside her phone, I kiss her again. I want her, and today's events have reminded me of how fleeting life can be. But when I settle on top of her, she freezes. I immediately roll onto my back.

"Sorry," she says. "I'm not in the mood tonight."

"That's fine."

"I can still get you off."

"I don't want you to feel like you owe me."

I think of my last relationship, when I was definitely the one with the lower libido, thanks to my meds. I'd put out even when I didn't want it; I felt I had to, in order to save what we had.

He broke up with me anyway.

"I'm not feeling pressured, don't worry," she says. "Even if I'm not in the mood for sexual gratification"—for some reason, the fact that she's using a five-syllable word turns me on—"I'll enjoy bringing you pleasure."

Many years ago, I dated someone who was very much a giver in the bedroom and got off on that, without me doing anything in return. I don't think this is quite the same, though.

"I mean it," she continues. "I want to be close to you. I want to see how you get yourself off...and help you. But no oral sex, and don't remove my shorts. And this isn't something I'm going to want all the time."

Her clear boundaries ease my mind.

I strip off my shirt, followed by hers, and roll back on top of her. She kisses me eagerly, but without the desperation that she sometimes has.

"Do you..." she begins. "Do you think of me when you touch yourself?"

"Yeah, but before we slept together, I was trying really hard not to."

"Same," she says, and my cock jerks in response.

She slips her hand into my underwear and touches me. I wish I could touch her too, but that's okay. I'll enjoy it all the more next time.

"You have toys, don't you?" she says. "I've seen them when you reach for the condoms."

I open the drawer, and after a moment of debate, I select a small butt plug and lube. "If it's okay with you..."

She nods. "I've always been curious."

"For use on yourself, or someone else?"

"Someone else." She slides off my underwear and leisurely strokes my cock while I hold myself above her. "Could you wear it while you fuck me?"

In addition to multisyllabic words, curse words are also really doing it for me right now, as long as they fall from her lips.

"I could." I've done it before, but not in a long time.

"You like how it makes you feel nice and full?"

I hiss out a breath. "Yeah."

Her lips curve into a smile, and I like that she's enjoying my reaction. I push into her hand. The fingertips of her other hand dig into my ass as I rut against her.

When she slides out from underneath me and grabs the plug that I've set on the bedside table, I tense in anticipation. She takes her time slicking it with lube. I focus on my breathing as she eases the tip of the plug inside.

"Like this?" she asks.

"Yeah." I exhale roughly.

Gently, she works the tip in and out before pushing the fattest part inside me. When I groan, she spanks me. Then she rolls me onto my back; I bend my legs. She plays with my ass for a little longer before turning her attention to my cock. After a few strokes, I'm rock hard. As she slowly jerks me off, she leans forward, her breasts swinging above my chest, and kisses me on the mouth. Again, her kisses feel a little different from when she's really turned on, but then she slides her hand lower, and I forget about what we're not doing; I'm focused on what she's doing to me.

I put my hand on top of hers and show her the exact rhythm I like. When she replicates it, it's way better than anything I could do by myself. Her warmth, her concentration, her legs on either side of my chest... She's looking after me, and I let her. She tugs my hair, pulling my head back to gain access to my neck, nibbling and licking my sensitive skin.

"I...not long," I bite out.

She rolls onto her side and picks up her pace.

"That's it," she says. "Yes, Evan..."

I hardly need encouragement, but I like it all the same.

I grunt as I spend on my stomach, and we lie there for a minute before she starts cleaning me up, taking a break every few seconds to press a kiss in one place or another.

"That was okay?" she asks me.

"More than okay," I tell her. "What about for you?"

"It was fun," she says, and I believe her. I can't imagine she'd lie about such things. At least not to me, not now.

Maybe I shouldn't feel special, but I do.

Jane falls asleep in my bed, but when I wake up at 6:45 the next morning—without the help of my alarm—I bolt up, feeling like something's not right. Instinctively, I look next to me.

I'm alone.

Terror seizes me, even as I tell myself to calm down. She's probably elsewhere in the house. It's not a big deal.

But even the idea of Jane being in her own bed fills me with worry. Did I do something wrong, and is that why she didn't want to sleep next to me?

I pad down the hall to her room. The door is ajar, and I carefully push it open. She's curled up on her side, the sheets around her waist.

I release the breath I was holding, then climb into bed behind her—her alarm will go off in a few minutes anyway. I wrap my arms around her, and she settles against me with a soft moan.

I love how she relaxes into me. How she looked so fucking studious while jerking me off last night. How she murmured to Watson when his bowtie wouldn't stay put.

I'm good at finding things to love about a person, but I'm not good at endings. With every breakup, I felt like I lost a little part of myself, no matter how hard I tried to paste a smile on my face and move forward.

With this marriage, I was supposed to put that behind me, all the ups and downs of falling in and out of love. It was supposed to be a steady relationship with a friend, someone whose quirks I already knew. But once again, I was wrong about a relationship.

Because I love my wife, and I'm too chickenshit to tell her.

I think back to our wedding night, when I was foolishly sad that I hadn't married for love. When I wondered if I should have waited until it happened to me again, then hoped against reason that it wouldn't end like it had so many times before.

I got what I wanted after all, but it doesn't feel good. I'm unsure of her exact feelings toward me, even as she releases a sigh of satisfaction in my arms.

Her alarm beeps. She turns it off, then rolls over.

"Did I snore last night?" I ask. "Is that why you came in here?"

"No," she says. "I just didn't want to disturb you as I read negative reviews online. Finally fell asleep around three."

There were times in my life when four hours would have been an average night's sleep, but it's not ideal. I will care for her the way she cared for me last night.

"Was something in particular keeping you up?" I ask.

She shakes her head. "Just happens sometimes."

I know what that's like. Still, it doesn't assuage my fears that I am, somehow, the one to blame, but I'm not going to push it.

"Were you worried when I wasn't in bed?" she asks.

"A little."

She pulls me close, like she can't help touching me, which is the same way I feel about her. It's often not sexual; I just want to hold her, reassure myself with her presence.

But I wonder how long this can last.

Chapter 21

Jane

I work later than usual to make up for yesterday, and just as I'm about to shut everything down for the weekend, my phone rings.

My father.

I'm functioning on less sleep than usual, and I'm so not in the mood for this, but I answer anyway, as I always do when he calls.

"Hi," I say, settling back in my comfy office chair.

"Hi, Jane. How are you?"

"Good."

Some people might feel comfortable being honest when their parents ask them such a question, but "honesty" hasn't described how I've interacted with my father for a couple of decades now.

Though in many ways I *am* good, aside from last night's poor sleep. My life has a nice rhythm, even if I'm unsure where this is all going.

"How is...Evan?" he asks. "Is that his name?"

Once again, I assure him that everything is good. "How are Suzanne and the kids?"

"Peyton just started university. I can't believe she's so grown up."

I wonder if he made a comment like that when I began university, which feels so long ago now. Or maybe he was too caught up with his new family to think about it much. I was a reminder of the past; they were the future.

I try not to let it bother me. For the most part, I've come to terms with the fact that my father isn't who I want him to be; there's no point hoping otherwise. It only leads to disappointment.

"Have you been..." Dad pauses. "Have you been keeping up with your pap smears?"

"Yes," I tell him. "I got one last year. No issues."

The question is awkward, but I appreciate it nonetheless. When HPV vaccines became available in Canada, Dad looked into how I could get one, and he asks about pap smears every few years now.

Other than giving me money, it's his only attempt to show he cares about me. He's not like Evan's parents, who talk to him regularly and load him down with food whenever they see him. Dad was so uncomfortable when I got my period that he couldn't even go to the feminine hygiene aisle with me, but I guess he feels an obligation to ask this question on occasion, given my mom died of cervical cancer.

"That's good," he says briskly. "The reason I'm calling is that I'm coming to Toronto for work." He gives me a date later this month. "I thought I could visit you at your new house. It'll be nice to catch up."

Nice to catch up. As though he's a not-so-close friend, rather than my goddamn father.

But I don't express my irritation.

"Sure," I say. "I can make us something for dinner."

We talk for a couple more minutes.

"I should go," he says. "By the way, Peyton asked for your phone number and address. I gave them to her. I hope you don't mind."

"No, that's fine." Though I'm confused, as she and I don't have a sisterly relationship.

After ending the call, I walk to my bedroom—where I slept last night for the first time in ages—and regard myself in the mirror above my dresser. Then I examine the photo of me with my parents, trying to figure out if I look much like my mother. Every time I do this, I conclude that I do. But maybe it's wishful thinking. I wonder if the similarity will fade as I age, as I become (hopefully) ten and twenty years older than she ever was.

I study my father in the picture. The man who, for a brief period of time, made me the center of his universe. But I no longer have that.

Could something similar happen with Evan?

Once again, I find myself wondering how different things would have been if my mother's cancer had been caught earlier. If she were still alive—or, at the very least, had lived until my twenties. I also wonder how much that shaped my feelings about being a woman. I say I'm a woman because that's what I've been told I am and I don't feel strongly about it, but it's not an important part of my identity. Would that be different if I had a mother? Or if my father hadn't pulled away when I went through puberty? Or does it have nothing to do with that? The rare times I speak to my father, I always end up pondering these sorts of things.

I pull my hair into a ponytail and head downstairs just as Evan comes in from his walk.

"Hey," he says. "I saw Skylar and Deena outside—they're heading to the hospital. Deena wanted me to thank you again for looking after Skylar. Also, I checked the mail."

There's a community mailbox at the end of our street. Evan is responsible for checking it, but he doesn't do it every day. We don't get much mail. But today, he passes me an envelope with a handwritten address.

"It's from Peyton," I say. Funny this arrived today.

I open the envelope as I head to the kitchen. I pull out a card with a pun about toast, and it takes me a moment to understand what I'm seeing.

A card to congratulate us on our wedding.

My first thought is that I'm surprised Peyton even knows how to send mail. I wasn't aware Gen Z ever did that. To be fair, it's not something I do much, either, though I remember being taught how to address an envelope in school.

But then I smile. Peyton took the time out of her day to do this. It's the only tangible acknowledgement of my marriage that I've received from my family, unless you count the check my dad gave me at Christmas.

"What is it?" Evan enters the kitchen.

In response, I hand him the card, and he chuckles at the pun.

"Should I hang it on the bulletin board?" he asks.

"Sure."

He tacks it up next to our calendar. Yes, we have calendars on our phones, but I like having a paper one as well.

"My dad called while you were out," I say. "He said he gave Peyton my contact info."

Evan pours himself a cup of water. His skin is glistening with sweat. "How is he?"

"Same old, I guess. He's coming to Toronto for work soon and wants to have dinner."

"When?"

I tell him the date, and he looks at our calendar.

"Crap," he says. "I'm supposed to go to Montreal for a few meetings. I was going to come back the following day, but I haven't booked the flights yet. I can see if—"

"No."

"You don't want me there?" He sounds a little disappointed.

"I would," I say honestly, "but I can manage on my own. I don't want to cause you any inconvenience."

He gives me a look. "You're my wife."

I've heard him call me that before, and it's just a simple statement of fact. But for some reason, the way he says it causes a stirring of pride and pleasure.

The word represents a commitment we made, a commitment to be a family—and now, it feels like more than what we initially intended.

"If you can make it work," I say.

He squeezes my hand. "I'll try to move something up so I can come back that afternoon."

"Thank you." To my embarrassment, I feel tears come to my eyes.

"Jane?" Evan doesn't tell me not to cry, for which I'm thankful, but through the tears blurring my vision, I can see the concern etched on his face.

"I don't know...I just...my dad didn't come to the wedding, despite months of notice, and you want to rearrange a trip because of a dinner."

It's more than that, but yeah, that's definitely part of it. I'm someone's priority now, and I'm not used to it.

A mix of emotions wells up inside me. I want to tell Evan that I love him, but it's been such a long time since I said those words to anyone. I'm afraid to do anything that might upset what we have. I don't know how fragile this is.

"You know you deserve so much better, right?" he says. "You deserve a father who actually shows that he cares for you."

I feel like I ought to defend my dad. Mention that he asked about pap smears.

But I don't.

"Yes," I say, "but deserving something doesn't mean you get it." I think of queer teenagers who get kicked out of the house by their parents. I also think of how my husband should have had the opportunity to marry for love...and didn't.

And yes, I do love him now, but I can't be sure of his feelings. I know he cares for me and has some level of attraction to me, but love? I don't know.

I wish I had more experience with such things.

He squeezes my hand again. "I'll get started on dinner."

Usually, I do the cooking, but this morning, after my poor night's sleep, he said he'd handle it today.

I pull out my phone to text Peyton. I'm pretty sure I have her number, and I'm also pretty sure I've never used it before. Indeed, I soon confirm there's no message history between us.

ME: Thank you for the card. I got it today.

ME: Where are you going to school?

I set my phone aside. Peyton, presumably, has better things to do on a Friday than text me. But before I have a chance to do some tidying in the living room, my phone buzzes.

PEYTON: Simon Fraser

PEYTON: no way was I staying in Calgary

I can't help chuckling. I wonder if it was more a need to see someplace different...or to get away from her parents. I'm not sure how long the drive is, but it's certainly not easy driving distance. A lot more than an hour or three.

ME: What's your major?

PEYTON: Biology. That's the plan, anyway.

PEYTON: I'm really sorry I couldn't come to your wedding. I had the money to fly to Toronto. But I can't get a credit card because I'm 17, which made it hard to book anything. Mom refused to book the flight for me and said I was too young to travel that far by myself.

How would she have the money? From a summer job? Part-time work? I assume she's not paying for school, but still.

And why would she have wanted to go to my wedding? Badly enough that she'd use her own money? We're not close.

I feel a wave of guilt that I didn't try harder with her.

Except she was a toddler when I started university, and my family moved out west a year later. I'm not close with my father or his second wife. And there were times when I *did* try harder with my half-siblings, but it didn't get anywhere.

I won't let the guilt get to me, but since she seems interested in a relationship now, I'll make an effort going forward.

I remember wanting a little sister when I was younger, and I wonder if my parents would have had another kid if my mom hadn't gotten sick. But by the time I did get a sibling, I was well into my teens, and it was one more thing that made me pissed off at my father. *You have time for a baby, but not for me?*

ME: That's ok. I understand.

PEYTON: Dad should have gone. Then I could have gone with him. Can't believe he missed your wedding because of a business trip.

PEYTON: But I have a friend at u of t and I'm hoping to get a job out there next summer. Don't tell mom and dad. Not yet. I'll visit you then.

A part of me delights in having a secret with a sibling. I've never had that before.

We chat for a little longer.

"Hey," Evan says, startling me. "Dinner will be ready in two minutes." He takes in my smile and gives me a curious look.

"Just texting Peyton," I say, as though it's a regular thing, rather than something I've never done before.

A few minutes later, I'm scarfing down fried rice. Evan isn't an especially good cook, but he's competent, which is more than can be said of some men, and it's nice to not have to cook all the time. Nice to chat about the mundane and not-so-mundane details of my day, rather than eating with my phone, like I used to do. I'd usually be in a cranky mood after a phone call with my father, but not today.

"I'm going to visit Max tomorrow," Evan says. "If you want to come, let me know, but I figured you'd be happy to have some time to yourself."

I wonder if he'd prefer to see his brother alone but felt he had to offer. I'm happy for him to have a relationship with his family separate from me—it's not like I feel excluded.

"I'll stay home," I tell him. "Maybe I'll go wild and...I don't know, bring Watson on a trip to the basement."

"He won't like it down there. It's too dark and gloomy."

"But *you* don't mind it? The deal was that you'd get the bigger bedroom if I got the upstairs office, but I've basically taken over your bedroom."

He gives me a look. "I'm not nearly as sensitive to these things as Watson, don't worry. Besides, I have feet, so I can move when I like. He's at the mercy of whoever brings him down there."

"That's a good point," I say, but my mind has drifted elsewhere.

It's rare for Evan to hang out with anyone without me. Does he find it too awkward, now that we live in the suburbs? We have a car, though. Does he feel guilty about leaving me alone?

"You know," I say slowly, "if you want to go out more often without me, I don't mind. Truly. Watson and Mr. Frog will keep me company. And if you don't want to drive, I can pick you up occasionally."

Though Evan doesn't really drink anymore—he did in university, but he doesn't like the way it makes him feel now—he does get high on occasion.

"I'll keep that in mind." He smiles, but it doesn't reach his eyes.

Later that night, as I'm lying in bed next to him, I think back to that smile. I didn't used to be such an expert on Evan's smiles, but that's changed.

He wasn't happy that I said he could go out by himself. But why? Does he feel like I'm trying to get rid of him?

And why doesn't he see friends more often?

I think of the blue bottle of antidepressants on the bathroom counter. He diligently takes them every day, despite the side effects.

Suddenly, it hits me.

Evan feels like he's doing people a favor by not making them spend time with him. When I encouraged him to go out without me, it felt like confirmation of that. He's still friendly with the people he encounters—he's gotten to know our neighbors better than I have, for example—but he keeps his distance.

He wasn't always like this. I know that much.

Oh, Evan.

My heart clenches as I curl closer to the man sleeping next to me, the man who wants to plan his flight so I don't have to face my father alone.

Maybe I'm wrong. I have clues, here and there, yet I can't be sure. I could ask him, but something in me recoils at the thought.

I don't know how to be close to someone.

And I don't know how he feels about me. Does he love me, but he's afraid of being rejected, afraid of upsetting the balance in our marriage?

I have no idea what it looks like when someone loves me. I've said "I love you" to two boyfriends, and neither of them said it back. I put my heart out there, as hard as it was for me, and the last time, I got a gentle, "I care about you, too." He was careful *not* to return the words I'd said to him. Maybe that's part of the reason I didn't even try to date for so long, and then I decided to forgo dating and simply get married.

I just don't fall in love in the right way.

There have been times in my life when I couldn't stand watching romances and romantic subplots. They usually portray something that doesn't quite make sense for me. Something that makes me feel broken, as foolish as that may sound. Figuring out that I'm demisexual—during my second relationship—made me feel a bit better about how I fall in love, but I still feel like I'm not doing it right.

Because these feelings weren't part of the plan. If I share the truth and it doesn't go well, there's so much I could lose. Waking up together. Morning coffee together. Pillow talk. A house that's half mine, with my own office. A home where I feel like I belong. A longtime friend.

He said he wouldn't have sex with anyone else, and maybe that means something—but not necessarily. He wasn't doing it before, and perhaps he just doesn't feel the need.

For the second night in a row, I can't sleep, so I get up and spend half an hour reading negative reviews of random products on Amazon.

This time, however, I return to Evan's bed when my eyes start to droop.

I don't want him to wake up alone.

Chapter 22

Evan

ON THE WAY TO visit Max, I stop at a bakery in Scarborough to buy mooncakes. The Mid-Autumn Festival is earlier this year than last year. My older brother prefers slightly different ones than I do, but I don't know what Kim likes.

Max's girlfriend isn't home when I get there.

"She's shopping," he says.

They've lived together for a few months, and I've only been here once before. It's not as perfectly neat as Max's place was when he lived alone, but it's still tidy.

In silence, he makes tea and cuts the lotus mooncake into wedges. He gives me one with more egg, which is what I like. He doesn't comment on it, though. Just does it.

As I sit with him at the kitchen table, the words I'd planned to say stick in my throat. I'd decided to tell him the truth about my marriage. Jane told Claudia, and she said it was okay if I told Max. But what I plan to tell my brother is probably a little different from what she told her friend earlier this year.

"Jane and I had a marriage pact," I say. "In 2020, when we were both lonely, we agreed...that if we were both still single by her thirty-third birthday...we would get engaged." I'm usually more fluent, but not today. Not about this.

Max arches an eyebrow, but he doesn't look as surprised as he ought to be. I guess he continued to have more suspicions about my marriage than I'd assumed

"I didn't think those pacts were ever serious," he says. "You could have broken it, but you didn't, even though I doubt you were secretly in love with her. Because...?"

"Because I was tired of getting dumped, and I couldn't keep doing it. I just couldn't."

"But you wanted to get married and buy a house?"

"Yeah."

There's a moment of uncomfortable silence, and I busy myself with my mooncake, which doesn't taste as good as it should; I can barely swallow.

"You didn't tell any of us," Max says. "So, why are you telling me now?"

I shut my eyes. "People don't respond well when you tell them that you've given up. This sort of marriage? It's just not..." I gesture feebly. I don't know what to say.

Max doesn't speak.

I open my eyes. It looks like he's waiting for me to continue.

"I know the engagement came out of nowhere," I say, "and you were hurt that I kept a big secret from you."

"I wasn't hurt."

Now it's my turn to arch an eyebrow—or at least try to do so. He's much better at it than I am. "I know you were, but you didn't refuse to act as a witness."

We lapse into silence once more.

"You're right," he says at last. "I would have told you not to give up. I would have told you that it took me a long time to find the right person, but eventually, I did."

"But I didn't *want* love. Well, in theory I did, but I'd started associating it with heartbreak. Going through that again...it didn't feel safe." I don't mention the issues that my depression—and the side effects of treatment—had on my relationships.

"Is this where you tell me that you've since fallen in love with her?" Max asks.

Ugh. Why does he have to be so smart?

"Unfortunately, yes." I drop my head into my hands. "Why do I keep doing this? I just can't learn. I should have realized that being in close proximity to someone else—someone I already liked as a friend—would make me more likely to fall for them."

"You're speaking as though this is a personality flaw."

"Because it is! There are probably tons of people I could fall in love with, if we got married and lived together."

"Do you really think that's true?" he asks.

"Are you trying to say she's special?"

"Maybe she is."

Against my will, I'm filled with hope. I swallow a mouthful of hot tea, as though that will dissolve my optimism.

"I don't think it's easy to fall in love with someone just because you live together," Max says. "Many relationships fall apart at that point. When you live with someone, they can get on your nerves in ways they never did before. You realize you're incompatible in one respect or another."

I glance around the apartment. Max said, just a few minutes ago, that he'd found the right person, but I can't help wondering...

"Kim and I are fine," he says, "but I've seen it happen to other people. Including you."

He's not wrong, though that was a while ago now.

Maybe this *is* different. But I've thought that many times before, haven't I?

"Are you sleeping together?" he asks.

"Yes."

"I assume you haven't told her how you feel?"

I shake my head. "I'm afraid it'll fuck everything up."

"You don't think she feels the same way?"

"I'm not sure, and even if she does..." I make some kind of gesture, meant to encompass all my failed relationships, though maybe I shouldn't think of them as "failed." Some of them might have been what I needed at the time. But they do have something in common: they all ended, and that ending hurt.

I can't bear to think of that happening with Jane.

"I still think you should tell her," Max says, his voice strangely gentle.

"Maybe if I wait long enough, this will go away."

"Perhaps." He sounds doubtful, and I don't blame him.

When he stands up to boil more water, he sets a hand on my shoulder.

"Not all hope is misplaced," he says.

When I get home, Jane comes downstairs to greet me. I catalogue it as one of the many things I like about being married that I would hate to lose. I hand her two red-bean mooncakes—that's what she prefers, and our tastes are in alignment.

"Thank you," she says. "How's Max?"

"Good."

"I asked Lana if she'd like to hang out next weekend, and she invited us for dinner on Saturday. What do you think? You up for that?"

"Sure." It's nice not to be the one making plans, and it feels like somehow, she knew that's what I needed.

I pull her close and press a kiss to her cheek.

When we visit Lana and Camila, I can't help thinking of the last time we saw them. So much has changed in the past several weeks. When they came to our house and brought us the charcuterie board, Jane had yet to spend a night in my bed. I wasn't afraid that confessing my feelings—like my brother thinks I should do—would fuck up my marriage.

Ah, a simpler time.

Yet as I watch Jane demurely sip her wine, I don't wish I could go back.

Instead, I want the impossible.

Chapter 23

Jane

When I wake up to my alarm on Wednesday morning, I'm alone in bed.

It's been weeks since I woke up by myself. Even the time I couldn't sleep and retreated to the other bedroom, I woke up with Evan holding me from behind.

But he got up an hour ago for an early flight, and apparently, he was quiet enough that he didn't disturb me.

As usual, I begin my day with the elliptical machine. When I come up from the basement, I start the coffeemaker and feel a strange pang in my chest.

It's not that I mind making my own coffee on a weekday. It's just weird that he's not here.

I sit outside as I drink my coffee. I read the news on my phone, since there's no one to talk to me and smile at me and squeeze my hand. When I turn to head into the house, I jump back in surprise. Yesterday, Watson sported a beret, but now, he's wearing a dark blue cape. Evan actually changed the penguin's outfit, even though he left before seven to catch a flight. Though why he owns a cape, I have no idea.

Later in the morning, my husband messages me to say he's arrived safely. I set my phone aside and return to work, but for some reason, it's harder to focus when I know he's not in the house with me, even though our offices are two floors apart.

Thursday morning, I wake up alone in Evan's bed again.

Yes, I slept in his bed last night, even though he's not here. It no longer feels like his bed, but *our* bed.

Once again, I head to the basement for my workout, then start the coffeemaker before my shower. After my shower, I take my coffee out to the patio. When I glance back, I half expect Watson to be wearing a different outfit, even though Evan is out of town.

Of course, Watson looks exactly the same as he did yesterday morning.

I rub my wedding band. I miss my husband a lot more than I should, considering he's been gone just over twenty-four hours, and I texted with him yesterday evening for twenty minutes. But I can't help missing all the ways he makes my life better.

After work, I decide to go for a walk and check the mail. Since there's nothing in our mailbox, it's a bit anticlimactic, but on the way back, I see Deena and Skylar on their driveway. Skylar is skipping. I lift up a hand in greeting, intending to keep walking, but then I figure…I can talk to them, right?

I come to a stop at the base of the driveway. "Hey!" My voice sounds unnaturally high. "I, um, wanted to check in and see how your father's doing."

Deena approaches me. "His surgery is scheduled for next month."

"Oh, that's good to hear."

"It's a struggle to make sure he follows all of the doctor's advice, though."

We talk for a few minutes, and Skylar shows me how she can skip with her arms crossed. She's in the middle of demonstrating her backward-skipping skills when my attention is distracted by a familiar Camry.

"Sorry," I say, "my mother-in-law just drove up." I dash over to the car as Lynne gets out of the driver's seat. Howie emerges from the passenger's side with a few bags in hand.

"Hi, Jane!" he says with a smile.

"Evan's not home. He's on a work trip to Montreal."

"We know. We thought we'd stop by with food so you don't have to cook for yourself."

As I unlock the front door and usher them inside, I struggle to wrap my head around those words. They came to visit *me*?

"We wanted to text you," Lynne says, "but we don't have your number. I asked Evan, but he hasn't replied—he's probably busy. If you want us to go—"

"No, no, you can come in." I feel like I ought to be a good host. At least the house is reasonably clean.

I head to the kitchen and put away the food, which is more than enough for two days. This is what I wanted, right? To feel like part of a family.

"Do you know how Evan's trip is going?" Howie asks.

"I talked to him last night." I start boiling water for tea and place some of the things they brought onto a plate. "His flight out was fine, and the work stuff..." We didn't talk about that much. "It seems to be going well."

"You could have gone with him," Lynne says. "Or traveled out on Friday. Spent the weekend in Montreal."

"You promised Evan you wouldn't bring it up again," Howie says.

"Did I say 'honeymoon'? No, I did not."

Oh my God. This again?

"My dad is visiting tomorrow evening," I say. It's the truth—and a good excuse.

"He's coming from Calgary to see you?" Lynne asks.

"Yes. Well, he's coming for work, and he's visiting me for dinner afterward."

Howie and Lynne exchange a look.

"Evan booked his flight so he'll be home for dinner," I say. "They'll finally be able to meet."

Lynne turns to me. "Is your father the reason you got married?"

I frown and reach for a pastry. "What do you mean? Why would I get married because of my dad? He didn't even come to the wedding."

She clucks her tongue. "I know, but I can't understand why my son married you."

I freeze.

"She didn't mean it like *that*." Howie turns to Lynne, and they exchange heated whispers in Cantonese.

"It's not that I don't like you." Her words aren't enough to reassure me. "But the engagement came out of nowhere, and I didn't believe you were in love. I know you're friends, I know you're fond of each other, so I thought maybe he was trying to help you out of a bad situation."

"Like what?" I ask.

"Like your father would force you to marry someone you hated. I don't know!"

"My dad would never force me to do anything. He barely even talks to me."

I watch my in-laws' expressions go from relieved to appalled. Though it can't be too much of a shock because, well, he didn't come to our wedding.

I wish Evan were here. I have no idea what to say, how to get out of this situation. I could tell them that I do love their son, but would they believe me now?

Fuck it. I'll just tell them the truth. It seems easier than dancing around the issue.

"We got married," I say, "because we were both tired of dating"—or, in my case, not dating—"but wanted to build a life with someone and buy a house."

Now it's Lynne's turn to frown. "That doesn't sound like Evan. He's a romantic."

"I know, but the breakups started to get to him." I pause. "Is that why you kept pushing the honeymoon? Because you knew we weren't...well...and thought we'd tell you the truth?"

"Ah, I don't know. Partly, but I also thought maybe if you went on a honeymoon, things between you would change."

"We are...getting closer," I admit.

"I'm glad. I know sometimes it happens that way, even if I knew it wouldn't happen to me in an arranged marriage."

"What?" I say before I can stop myself. I hope that didn't sound rude. I'm just flummoxed by her comment.

Lynne hesitates. "I was supposed to marry someone else. The son of my parents' friends. He was a few years older than me, and I knew, my whole life, it was what they wanted. But I hated him. Even as a boy, he was horrible, and when he grew up, he was even worse."

I don't know how to respond. Does Evan know about this?

"So, you said no and your parents listened?" I ask, even though I'm pretty sure they didn't.

She chuckles without mirth. "No, I fell in love with someone else and ran away with him the week before I was supposed to get married."

I gape at her. I struggle to picture this version of Lynne, forty years ago, even as she touches her husband's shoulder.

"Because of my experience," Lynne says, "I never told my sons who they should marry, even as they reached their thirties with no weddings in the family. Or when…"

"When Evan came out?" I supply.

"I know we didn't react the best."

He told them when he was fourteen, naively—as he later put it—believing that since they were in favor of same-sex marriage, they wouldn't respond poorly. But some parents are okay with such things for other people, just not for their own kids.

Fortunately, that wasn't the case with Evan's parents. No, it simply hadn't occurred to them that this would directly affect their family. They sat there in stunned silence as Evan freaked out, until Max—who was seventeen and already knew—told them what to say.

So, yes, it could have gone better, but it also could have gone so much worse. And in the two decades since then, his parents have been supportive.

"He could have married someone of any gender," Lynne says. "We would have been fine with it, but your engagement…it worried me. He never told me you were dating, and I knew he was making excuses. But I liked you, and he seemed so certain. And now, I understand. I won't ask about your honeymoon anymore. You don't have to tell him that we know."

"I'll tell him," I say, feeling weird about keeping the details of this conversation a secret. "Not until he comes back from Montreal, though." I'd prefer to do it in person, and I'll see him tomorrow—it's not like I'll have to wait long.

Howie nods. "I'm sure your father was also very surprised by your engagement…" He trails off, presumably realizing this wasn't the case.

It's like they can't comprehend barely having a relationship with your adult child. It's beyond their imagination.

I swallow. "I'm glad Evan has a...a loving family. I used to long for one."

Howie's eyes are misted with tears. I wonder if I shouldn't have said that, but then he pushes the platter of sweets toward me.

And when Lynne stands up a few minutes later, she gives me a hug.

I'm pretty sure that if my mom were alive, she wouldn't be much like Lynne. The young mother of my memories has a different personality, and though some of it might be thanks to a faulty memory, to the way we edit events in our mind after they happen, I believe there's a kernel of truth in my memories.

I don't think they'd be alike, but I think they'd get along, and as she pulls back, I feel I have a better sense of what it's like to have a mother as an adult.

After scarfing down dinner—it's a good thing I don't have to cook, because I'm really not in the mood—I call Claudia to talk about Evan's parents, as well as how much I miss my husband.

"Are you going to tell Evan how you feel about him?" she asks.

I regard my friend's face on the screen of my phone. "I don't know."

Claudia, bless her, doesn't try to give me advice. I couldn't handle it right now. There are only so many feelings and difficult conversations I can manage in one day.

"But I do think you should go on a honeymoon," she says, "or another trip. You haven't been anywhere this year, and you deserve a holiday. With me, if not with Evan."

"You've already come to Toronto. I could go out west, or we could meet in the middle—"

"Winnipeg? I've never been."

"I don't know much about Winnipeg, but I'll look into it."

"Already on it," she says. "We could go to the mint?"

"Sure. Why not." As long as I get to spend time with her. "Although..."

"What is it?"

"If I visit you in B.C., I could also visit Peyton. She sent me a card and wishes she'd been allowed to go to my wedding."

We've texted a few times since then. She sent me a meme that she thought I'd find funny. I didn't understand it, but I appreciated it nonetheless. I also discovered that snail mail is some kind of cool, old-fashioned thing in her group of friends. Like how some people in my generation got into records? I don't know.

"Okay," Claudia says. "Think about it and let me know. If we're going to Winnipeg, we should probably do it soon. Before it gets too cold."

"Good point."

I'm looking forward to seeing her again. It'll be fun. And now seems like a good time to tell her something that I've never told her before.

I tighten my grip on my phone and take a deep breath. "I love you."

I know she'll understand how I mean it. Not at all romantic, but maybe it's practice for when I do say it in a romantic way. Still, it's nerve-racking to put the words out there.

But for the first time in my adult life, they're returned.

"I love you, too."

Chapter 24

Evan

After my final meeting, I head to Montréal-Trudeau Airport. I don't like airports and flying—it stresses me out—but today, I'm mostly filled with excitement. It's a short flight, I don't have to go through customs, and soon, I'll get to see my wife again.

But then I look at the departures board.

"No, no, no," I mutter under my breath.

My flight is delayed by over an hour. It's leaving at the time I was supposed to arrive.

I scan the board for another flight to Toronto with the same airline—maybe there's an empty seat on an earlier flight and they'll be able to change my ticket. Unfortunately, the only flight I can find leaves in five minutes, and there's no way I'll make it.

"*Shit*," I say, not quite as quietly.

I was supposed to be home by six so I could be there when Jane's father arrived. Even if traffic prevented me from getting there before he did, I was at least supposed to be there before dinner. I'm doubtful that will happen now, especially since the next time I look at the board, the departure has been pushed back by another fifteen minutes.

I pull out my phone and see that in my rush to get to the airport, I missed a text about the delay. Not that it would have helped me.

Well, here you are. Screwing up again.

I do my best to shut down the voice in my head. I hate the feeling of being another man who's disappointed Jane, even if a flight delay isn't my fault. But travel issues aren't good for my negative self-talk.

A part of me feels like I should have known this would happen, as unreasonable as that is. Though given everything I had to do today, it's not like I could have booked an earlier flight anyway.

The last few times I've flown, everything went according to plan. I can't believe this is the time there are problems. I hate feeling so helpless.

Goddammit.

I've already checked in online, and I don't have to check any luggage. Since I was only gone for two nights, I didn't need to bring much. Once I go through security, I head to my gate and take a seat. I send Jane a selfie of me wearing a black face mask and looking sad.

> EVAN: My flight has been delayed by over an hour. Start dinner without me.

> EVAN: I'm so sorry

It's not that I don't believe she can handle a dinner with her father, but I want to be there for her. And I do want to meet him, even if I don't think much of him.

Plus, I really want to see my wife. Even though we haven't been sharing a bed for all that long, it was still strange waking up in a hotel without her. It didn't feel right. We've texted a little, but I want to tell her about my trip and hear what she's been up to. Apparently, my parents stopped by with food yesterday, but I don't know much more than that. I wish she could have been here with me. I've been to Montreal a number of times before, but with her, I would have been more interested in walking around the city and trying new restaurants.

My leg bouncing up and down, I mindlessly scroll through the news, barely seeing the words. There's no point in trying to do anything productive—I can't think clearly enough for that now. I just need to get through the wait; I'll feel better once we're in the air.

> JANE: I hope it doesn't get delayed any further. Sitting in an airport sucks.

> JANE: I know you feel bad about not being here, but it's not your fault. I understand.

She has a good sense of what's going through my mind right now, and hearing it from someone else? That calms me a little.

Since she has work to do this afternoon, I don't say much more. I stare at my wedding band and think of the matching one on her hand. I've only worn the ring for about two months, but already, it feels like such an integral part of me.

I take a deep breath and will the plane to come faster.

Chapter 25

Jane

"Peyton is at Simon Fraser," Dad says. "Did I tell you?"

"No," I say, "but she did." I cut up my chicken but don't put any in my mouth. I don't have an appetite.

My father eats as though he's ravenous, and he talks in between bites without paying attention to my responses. "She's studying biology. Why couldn't she do that at U of C? So much closer."

"Mm."

When I was a year older than her, you moved to the other side of the country. You never cared about being close to me when I was in school.

We're at the kitchen table, since Evan and I still haven't gotten around to purchasing a dining room table for when we have visitors. I wish I could eat with him instead. It would be much more enjoyable.

Every word my father says is a reminder of what he didn't do for me.

Absently, I wonder whether he ever bragged about me when I was Peyton's age. Maybe he did, even if he had nothing to do with any of my successes. But I can't imagine him wishing that I stayed home for university. Instead, I felt like he was glad to get rid of me.

"She said something about ecology." He makes a dismissive gesture. "Hopefully, we can convince her to write the MCAT."

I imagine Peyton rolling her eyes at this comment. I feel a moment of regret that my dad never tried to convince me to do things I didn't want to do, as ridiculous as it is. Maybe that would have made me feel like he cared.

"Kay is so smart," he says. "Though he doesn't want me to call him that anymore. He's on the badminton team at school..."

I tune out as he talks about Kaden's achievements.

I didn't think it would be different this time. I really didn't. I'm too old and jaded for that. But allowing him to visit might be proof that some small part of me still hoped. Or did I just want to show him that I belong somewhere?

Being around him today feels different than it did in the past.

"I thought your husband was going to be here?" Dad says. "I can't believe you're old enough to have a husband."

"I'm thirty-three," I say tightly, because he might have forgotten.

A strange look passes over his face. Perhaps he's realized I'm older than my mother ever was? Who knows.

"Evan had to go to Montreal for work," I say. "He was supposed to be back for dinner, but his flight got delayed." He texted me while I was cooking to say he was leaving Pearson, but it'll still take a while for him to get here.

My father asks a couple of questions about Evan's job before saying, "I really am sorry I missed your wedding, but it couldn't be helped."

And that does it for me. I can't take any more of this.

"Oh really," I mutter. "With a few months' notice, there was *nothing* you could do? You *had* to miss my wedding, just like you had to miss my graduations?"

Normally, I wouldn't talk back; I'd murmur a few words and hope it would be over soon. His behavior is nothing new, after all. But now I understand, more than I ever did before, how much better I deserved, and for some reason, I can't just shut down like I usually do.

"Yet here you are," I say, "telling me that you go to Kaden's badminton games."

"Do not bring him—"

"I'm not mad at him. I'm mad at *you*."

He looks genuinely baffled.

"I haven't been anything close to a priority to you," I say, "in over twenty years. It started before you even met Suzanne, so I know it wasn't just you forgetting about me once you had a new wife and kids, though that probably didn't help."

"You were always so independent. You didn't need me like they did."

I snort. "I was independent because I had to be. I didn't have a choice."

"You started pushing me away—"

"Like all teenagers. It's normal. Yet you just gave up, once I wasn't a cute little girl anymore, and you pushed me away, too. You were the parent, not me, but you didn't act like it. And now I'm expected to listen while you talk about the relationship you have with your younger children? No. I don't owe you that. You weren't there when I needed you."

"Like when?" He still sounds baffled.

It's not like I truly expected this confrontation to lead anywhere good, but I had to get it out. Maybe I also thought there'd be half-hearted promises to do better. I don't know; it's hard to sort through everything churning inside me.

"Like when I got my period, for example."

Unsurprisingly, he looks uncomfortable. "What did you expect from me? It's not fair that you didn't have a mother, but I'm a man, I don't know these things."

"You didn't even try! You didn't need to be perfect, but you should have been there. So many times over the years, you just weren't present. Not even for my fucking wedding!"

"Don't swear, Jane."

"Now you want to parent me?" I know I sound like a teenager, but I can't seem to help it. I drop my voice. "Once upon a time, you were a pretty good dad. After Mom died, you tried your best for a few years. We had no other family here, and I looked up to you. You were my world. And then... Were you like this with Peyton as she got older? I don't think it was quite the same, maybe because you had her mother to guide you. But why couldn't you have let her come to my wedding? She wanted to be there, and it meant so much to me..."

Where am I going with this? I don't even know. I'm just spewing out all the things that had been left unsaid for so long. It probably won't help, but it's a relief to actually say what's on my mind.

And then I hear a key in the lock.

Chapter 26

Evan

"You must be Evan." Jane's father rises from the table to shake my hand. He has salt-and-pepper hair, and he's shorter and slighter than my own father.

The atmosphere is tense, and my wife's hand trembles on the table. She's abandoned her chicken, and it's not like her to leave food half-eaten. Her dad's plate, in contrast, has multiple bones.

What did he do to her?

I curse the plane for not taking off on time. I should have been here.

"Nice to meet you," I say, though my tone must convey that I certainly don't think this is *nice*.

After releasing the older man's hand, I glance back at my wife, and when her eyes meet mine, I know what happened. She got angry and told her father all the things she's kept bottled up, and his response was, once again, disappointing.

I can't remember the last time I raised my voice, but I'd relish the opportunity to show how little I think of him, this man who wasn't the father that my wife needed. It kills me to think of how much he failed her.

However, I know Jane wants to fight this battle by herself. So, I'll support her, but I won't interfere.

"Your food is on the counter," she says to me.

I lift an upside-down bowl to reveal two grilled chicken thighs. I dump some salad on the plate, then sit down at the table. I'm starving, though I'm not in the mood to eat now.

Under the table, Jane's right hand finds my left, and she squeezes. I squeeze back.

She doesn't say anything more.

After a long silence, her father stands up. "I should get going."

My wife appears relieved by this comment, so I stand up with her, and we follow him to the door. He puts on his shoes and grabs his bags, then hesitates with his hand on the doorknob.

"Take good care of her," he says to me, and I wonder if he has any regrets. He ought to, but I'm not sure he does.

He leaves without waiting for us to respond.

Once he's gone, Jane starts to tremble, and I wrap her in my arms. It's a relief to finally touch her properly after being away for two nights.

"I've got you," I say. "I'm here. What do you need?"

She just burrows against me. Seeing her like this makes me ache.

Once she's stopped shaking, I lead her to the living room, where I sit down on the couch and pull her close. I don't want to stop touching her, and she seems to feel the same way.

"He was bragging about his other kids," she says at last. "He talked about going to Kaden's badminton games. Wishing Peyton hadn't decided to go to university away from home. I couldn't take it anymore, after he didn't come to our wedding." Tears start leaking out of her eyes. "He said I was so independent, I didn't need him, I pushed him away as a teenager... I told him I just wanted him to try."

She looks uncharacteristically fragile, and it wells up in me suddenly, this need to tell her how I feel. The need for her to know that even if her father doesn't love her the way he should…

I don't wipe her tears away, but when sobs are no longer racking her body, I push her damp hair back from her face and say, "I love you."

If she takes those words to mean a platonic love of close friends, that's fine. I just know it's important for her to hear it. Her dad hasn't been there for her, but I will be.

She raises her head. "Until yesterday, nobody had said that to me other than my mom."

"Yesterday?"

"When I was talking to Claudia."

"What about your exes?"

She shakes her head. "I said it, but they didn't say it back."

"Oh, Jane." I know how hard it would be for her to take that risk, this woman who felt unwanted in her own family.

At the same time, I'm keenly aware that she hasn't returned my words.

But that's okay. I can manage.

She traces my eyebrows with her finger. My jaw. Then her finger moves down to my collarbone. I can barely breathe, but I don't tell her to stop. I crave her touch. Two and a half days? That was far too long to be without it.

"But before I say it to you," she whispers, "I need to know how you meant it."

I feel lightheaded. "I…"

I can tell her the truth. But she's experienced a lot of emotional upheaval today, and I don't want to make it worse, and what if…

At my hesitation, the light dims in her eyes.

And I know. I just know.

I know this is different from anything I've felt before, and I know she feels it, too, though there's a part of me that can't quite believe it.

"I meant it in every way," I say. "I love you, I'm in love with you, I can't imagine I'll ever stop loving you. I didn't marry you for romantic reasons, but now, I feel like I did, even though I'd sworn it off. I was afraid to tell you because it wasn't part of our deal...but I do."

Feeling overwhelmed, I shut my eyes, but then I feel her hand on my cheek. Her thumb gently strokes my skin.

"I love you," she says, "in exactly the same way."

Then she kisses me, this wonderful person who's building a life with me. Who looks amazing whether she's cutting the grass or doing my makeup.

Who *loves* me.

Joyous laughter escapes my lips as I open my eyes. When my gaze lands on something across the room, I laugh again. At some point while I was gone, Watson changed his outfit. He was wearing a cape when I left, but now, he's got a little crown fashioned out of yellow paper.

Jane smiles. "I love all the little things you do for me. All the ways you make me feel cared for. I really missed you when you were gone, even if your trip was short. I woke up alone and drank coffee alone—and I wished you were there with me."

"You're not going to get sick of me?"

"I can't imagine I would. I might have only felt this way for a few weeks, but I've known you for a long, long time—and I'm sure."

Before, I wondered if I'd be able to fall in love with lots of different people, if we were in close proximity like this. Max didn't think that was true, and now, I'm positive he was right.

Sometimes, you just know.

I pull her close. "I love you so much." I want to say it again and again.

And I will.

Chapter 27

Jane

When I wake up on Saturday morning, Evan is next to me in bed. I smile, and that smile broadens as I remember last night.

My husband loves me.

Until yesterday, I didn't know what it was like to love someone like this and have that love returned. Not everyone wants this kind of relationship, but I always did, even if I sometimes pretended otherwise.

And now, I finally have it.

My mood darkens a little as I remember my father's visit, which quashed the silly hopes that I tried not to have. It was good to get it out, though, and I feel like that will help me move on.

Will I still talk to him a couple of times a year? I haven't decided, and that's okay. But I know I want a relationship with Peyton. I'm not sure exactly what it will look like, since we've only just start connecting outside of my rare visits to Calgary, but I'm looking forward to getting to know her beyond my father's bragging. Maybe I'll start talking to Kaden, too.

One step at a time.

I know my life might seem small to some people. I don't go out or travel a lot. I don't have a career that I find especially fulfilling. But at thirty-three, I'm happily married and own a house, and that seems like enough of a miracle.

Not wanting to wake up Evan yet—it's only eight and he had a long day—I reach for my phone and notice that I got a text late last night.

DAD: Your mother would be proud of you.

A number of people have said that to me over the years, despite the fact that most of them had never met her. But coming from my father, it's different.

What was their marriage like?

I hope you were happy, Mom.

In my memories, except those at the very end, she's always smiling, but that doesn't necessarily mean she was happy with him.

It briefly occurs to me that my father's words could be sarcastic, but I don't think they are. I think he means them. Yet it's not lost on me that he invokes my mother without saying *he's* proud of me.

I pad out of the room to grab the framed picture of my family. I return to Evan's bedroom—our bedroom—and set it on the bedside table. Next to me, he stirs.

"Hey." He pulls me close, my chest against his.

We did a lot of snuggling last night, but I still want more. There's nothing quite like mornings in bed with him.

I roll onto my side. As I adjust my position, I feel a certain part of him responding. I wiggle my ass against him. In turn, he slips his hand under the hem of my shirt and cups my breast, giving it a squeeze. Then his hand lazily wanders between my legs.

I made a strange noise in the back of my throat, and I can feel his rumble of laughter. He slides his finger inside me, and his thumb brushes my clit. Gently, just the way I like it.

When he withdraws, I moan in protest. He makes quick work of my clothes before sliding down my body and setting his mouth on me. I moan for an entirely different reason, and he lifts his head and gives me a wicked smile that I find endearing.

I am immensely fond of him.

When I grip his hair and push his face down, he laughs and gets back to work.

Sex used to be more complicated for me. In one way or another, it seemed like my feelings toward it weren't quite what people wanted them to be—and my body was so damn *picky*. But with Evan, it doesn't feel like that. It never did, not even at the beginning when we were figuring out what the other person preferred.

And now, it just feels right.

He laps at me, his tongue moving over my pussy, and when I'm almost there, he stops.

I give him a thoroughly unimpressed look and smack his ass, which I suspect is what he wanted. He also knows that I usually prefer to finish later, even if it frustrates me.

As he takes off his clothes and reaches into his bedside table for supplies, I reach over to my table and turn the picture away. Heh.

In addition to the condom packet and lube, Evan holds up the butt plug that I used on him before, and I nod. He passes it to me, and when our hands brush, I feel a spark of electricity.

Once I've got a proper grip on the plug, I lube it up, and he gets on all fours and I tease his opening, his whimpers urging me on. Finally, I push it all the way in, and he groans.

He raises himself up on his knees, and I join him, my chest against his. He puts one hand on my cheek and the other on my back before kissing me like he can't get enough of me. I thrust my fingers into his adorably mussed hair and return the kiss in exactly the same way. His erection is pressed between us, and God, I want him.

I lightly push him backward so that he's lying on his back. He crosses his arms behind his head, and I admire him for a moment before stealing another kiss. When I slide down his body and take his cock in my mouth, he groans again and throws an arm over his eyes. I cup his balls as I shift my mouth to his inner thigh. I suck on his skin, drawing it into my mouth, and nibble.

"Jane..." It's the first thing he's said in a long time, and it feels like he's imbuing my single-syllable name with so many emotions.

Love. Wonder. Desperation.

Once I'm satisfied I've done enough to leave a mark, I roll on a condom and slowly sit on his cock, moaning when I've taken all of him inside me. He really is just the right size. I ride him leisurely, and he smiles up at me. Then I roll my hips hard against him and pick up the pace, in a way that has made him lose his mind in the past—and I'm not disappointed. He's practically flailing beneath me, and I feel like the most powerful person in the world. How am *I* able to do this to him?

A moment later, I'm on my back, not quite sure how I got here, and he's above me, urgently thrusting. My hands are all over him; I feel like I can't touch him enough.

"Jane," he says again, then thrusts into me one more time...and holds.

Once his orgasm has ebbed, he pulls out of me and immediately slides down my body. Two fingers in my pussy and a gentle suck on my clit are all it takes for me to pull his hair and cry out his name.

After we clean up, we return to bed. It's nine o'clock, and I'm usually up by this time on the weekend, but I don't care.

"I love you," I tell Evan again, and he smiles at me like it's the greatest news ever, even though he's known it for...well, about twelve hours.

"I love *you*," he says.

He pushes aside the sheet and brushes his fingers over the faint bruise on his inner thigh. He hisses out a breath.

Yeah, I was right. He totally likes hickeys.

We lie there in silence, his fingers running through my hair, for a few minutes before he says, "So about having children..."

I release a startled laugh.

"Have you changed your mind?" he asks.

"No, but I still think we should wait until next summer. I want some time just for us."

"I agree."

"Are you sure?" I ask. "You weren't going to suggest we start trying right away?"

"Not going to lie, a part of me wants to, but I think waiting is the right call. I just wanted to check in, since we haven't actually talked about it for a while."

Even though we're not trying yet, having kids now feels more real than it ever did before. It's not a hazy image in my brain, but something I can really imagine happening...with him.

"Just one thing," I say. "Don't get me wrong, I have faith you'll be a good parent, but promise that if something happens to me, you won't do what my dad did. I'm not saying you should never remarry, but I hate to think of our kids feeling like they aren't wanted, or don't have a family, or..."

He doesn't say that nothing will happen to me, which I appreciate. I know he wants to, but he understands this is important to me. While I don't expect the unlikely to occur, I still feel the need to discuss it. Just in case.

"I promise," he says solemnly.

We stay in bed for another half hour. Then Evan gets dressed and heads downstairs to make coffee while I jump in the shower.

And as I stand under the spray, I think, *I feel in love just right.*

After I sit down on the back patio with my coffee—which Evan has poured into a new penguin mug that he got in Montreal—I turn to look at Watson. He's wearing a pink scarf.

"What do you want to do today?" Evan asks.

"I didn't have any particular plans," I say. "Though I do need to cut the grass at some point this weekend. Probably won't have to do that too many more times."

"I'd offer to cut it, but you seem to enjoy it."

"I do."

"And truth be told, I like watching you. I found myself staring at your ass while you were cutting the grass several weeks ago, and I felt guilty about it."

"You don't have to feel guilty anymore," I say, but then I frown.

"What is it?"

"I just remembered. When your parents were here, I told them the truth about why we got married. Your mom said, 'I can't understand why my son married you—'"

"*What?*" Evan is pissed on my behalf, and I admit, it's rather gratifying.

"She assured me that she likes me; she just knew we weren't in love, and she thought maybe a honeymoon would help us grow closer. I suggested that things might be changing, but that's it. I'm sorry. I didn't know what else to say."

"I can't believe she brought it up when I wasn't there."

"She was asking about my father's visit and...yeah."

He touches my shoulder. "Don't worry, I totally understand why you said something. I also confessed the truth to Max. I needed to talk to someone because I wasn't sure what to do, whether to reveal my feelings to you. He said I should."

It is a little weird that more people know than we'd initially intended, but it's hard to care too much when I'm so happy to be with Evan.

"Your mom also told me," I say, "that she was supposed to marry someone she hated—the son of her parents' friends—but she ran away with your father instead."

Based on Evan's expression, this is news to him. I wonder if any of his brothers know.

"I...well, that does explain a few things," he says at last. "About my grandparents, as well as a few other conversations I've heard over the years. If I saw it in a drama, I'd find the whole thing rather romantic." His lips curve upward, and another wave of fondness rushes over me. I'm lucky to just be sitting here, drinking coffee with my husband. "But thinking of how they must have pressured her...it's appalling."

"Were you close with your mother's parents?"

He shakes his head. "They didn't live here, and even when we went to Hong Kong, we wouldn't spend a lot of time with them."

I reach out and take his hand. I feel like I'm smiling for no reason, which isn't like me. But it's not for no reason: I'm in love with my husband and he's in love with me. I never thought this would happen, yet it did.

It still feels new and special and miraculous. I know every-thing won't always feel as easy as it does now, but I hope I won't forget how lucky I am. While I'm sure we'll have challenges, I feel good about our ability to face them together.

"Let's go on a honeymoon," I say. "I want to take a trip to see Claudia this fall, and we could combine it with that, or we could go somewhere else. If you can get the time off."

"If it's not more than a week, it shouldn't be a problem. Maybe somewhere to enjoy the fall colors? New England, or up north?"

Long after the coffee is finished, we sit in our backyard, mak-ing plans for our future.

That afternoon, Evan and I do something we've never done together before: we go for a walk around our neighborhood. He goes for walks every day, and I've been for the occasional walk, too, but we've never done it together, our hands clasped. The leaves on a few trees are turning red and gold, and it's a perfect afternoon outside.

As we walk through a small park, a little pup on a long leash runs up to us, and Evan crouches down to pet it. I open my mouth to protest—why is he petting a strange dog? Then I realize he knows this dog and has pet it many times before. He introduces me to the dog, Peaches, and then the owner.

"You didn't tell me about Peaches," I say to my husband, once the pup is out of earshot.

"Was I supposed to?"

"Yes! You're supposed to tell me about all the dogs you see each day. I thought that was one of the perks of marriage."

"I'll be sure to do that from now on."

"See that you do." I might be speaking in a comically huffy tone, but I lean forward and plant a kiss on his lips.

We soon encounter two more dogs; Evan knows one of them, but not the other. We also encounter two humans unaccompanied by dogs, and Evan introduces me to them.

As we turn onto another street, Evan points out a house that had beautiful pink hydrangeas earlier in the year. He waves at a woman in her front yard and tells me that she's a high school teacher. Apparently, while going for his daily walks, my husband has been getting to know the neighborhood in a way that I haven't. It reminds me of something I want to ask him.

"Remember when I said you could go out without me? You seemed a little uncomfortable with the conversation, and I was wondering..." I keep my tone gentle. "Why don't you have as much of a social life as you used to? I worry you feel like you're doing people a favor by not texting them and making plans."

Evan gives me a startled look and stops walking. "What makes you say that?"

"Sorry, I could be wrong. It was just a feeling."

Though as soon as I say it, I'm positive I'm right.

He continues walking but at a slower pace. His smile doesn't reach his eyes. "It's weird to hear someone say that out loud, rather than inside my head. It sounds more logical in here."

That this kind, wonderful man could ever think such things about himself...

"When my depression was at its worst and it was difficult to see people—you know, the pandemic—I gave up on many friendships."

"But not ours," I say.

"No. After all, we had a marriage pact, which helped me imagine a future for myself when that was a difficult thing to do."

My heart clenches. I can't put everything I'm feeling into words, so I settle for squeezing his hand.

"Though sometimes, I felt bad about possibly shackling you to me. Not anymore, don't worry." He sighs. "Yeah, I should reach out to some friends. A few people, though, I think it's best to let go of. But not all of them."

"I'm happy you're here with me now."

"Me, too."

We feel safe to be vulnerable with each other, and that's a lovely thing.

By the time we return to the house, Evan is sweaty, even if it's not very warm. I kiss him right inside our front door, and as I do, I think of how beautiful a word it is.

Our home. *Our* family. *Our* love.

Once upon a time, I felt like I didn't have a real home or family. But now, I'm putting down roots where I belong.

With Evan Mok.

Epilogue

Evan

I've forgone my usual walk today, but it's for a good reason: I had to pick up a birthday cake before the bakery closed.

As I drive toward our house, I pass the community mailbox. It occurs to me that I ought to check the mail, just in case, even though I did it yesterday. When I find an envelope for Jane, I'm very glad I stopped.

I arrive home a couple of minutes later. Skylar is attempting to roll a snowball in the small amount of snow we got last night—our first of the season. I wave at her before heading inside my and Jane's house. After taking off my winter clothes, I walk to the kitchen, where my wife is drinking a cup of water. She's wearing yoga pants and a cozy sweater, and she looks utterly lovely. I set the bakery box on the counter and give her a quick kiss.

"You can take that scarf off now," she teases.

I made sure I wore a scarf during my earlier Zoom meeting and when I went to the bakery, but she's right: I don't need to hide my hickey when it's just the two of us. I unwind the scarf from my neck, and I groan as she brushes her fingers over the small mark.

I can't let myself get too distracted, however. I still have a dinner to cook, but first, I go to the next room and tie the scarf around Watson's neck. It sort of clashes with his party hat, but

I have a feeling he doesn't mind. Besides, it has the desired effect of making Jane chuckle, and that's the most important thing.

When I return to the kitchen, she opens the box. Like the one I got her exactly a year ago, it has words written in chocolate, but this time, they say, "Happy Birthday."

"Is it the same as the bottom tier of our wedding cake?"

"Since your birthday is also the anniversary of our engagement—and you really like this cake—I thought it was appropriate. More appropriate and elegant than, I don't know, a cake that looks like a hamburger." I pull her close. "Happy thirty-fourth birthday, Jane."

I've already wished her that more than once, but she deserves to hear it again.

The past couple of months have been wonderful, to put it mildly. I'd originally expected our marriage to be comfortable and convenient, but it's so much more than that. Jane and I go to sleep in the same bed every night now, our favorite wedding picture hanging on the wall opposite the bed. I hope that one day, her old room will be our child's room.

I pull out the envelope from under the cake box. "I checked the mail on the way home."

"It's from Peyton." Jane opens the envelope and smiles as she shows me a birthday card.

My wife hasn't spoken to her father since his visit in September, but she's been keeping in touch with Peyton, and she took her out for dinner when she went to B.C. last month.

I didn't go on that trip with her, but we did manage a trip together in October. We went to a resort up north and spent three nights in a honeymoon suite. It was lots of fun. We spent a fair bit of time in bed and in the tub, but we also enjoyed the leaves. I appreciate that she doesn't doubt my passion for her, even if I'm not always trying to jump her.

Her phone buzzes. She takes a quick look, then shows me the screen. It's a text from my mother, wishing her a happy birthday. The other day, my mom suggested that she and my dad could take us out for dinner today if Jane wanted, but I consulted with my wife, and we agreed to do it some other time. I'm glad I can share my family with Jane, but I'm also glad she's become closer with Peyton.

She deserves to have as many loving people in her life as she can.

That Sunday, we go to my parents' house for dinner. My parents have put up their Christmas tree, and maybe that's why I can't help thinking of last Christmas's family gathering as Jane and I sit on the couch in the living room.

How much difference a year can make.

Leo and Yvonne are in the kitchen with my father. My mother and Jon are in the living room, but Max and Kim still aren't here yet, which is odd. Max is rarely the last to arrive.

A moment later, I hear the front door open, and while everyone else stays seated, I go to greet my brother. He's whispering something to Kim and doesn't immediately see me. Her cheeks are pink. Whether it's from the December cold or another reason, I'm not sure.

I suddenly have a feeling that Max did what he told me he was going to do. When I notice Kim is keeping her left hand in her pocket, my suspicion is confirmed.

"Congratulations," I murmur, holding him back as Kim enters the living room.

His lips quirk up.

I hope he'll be as happy in marriage as I am, but I'll save any further words for the official announcement, which I assume will be in the next few minutes.

As I reenter the living room, I can't help looking at Jon. Everyone is coupled up aside from him. He acts like he's content with hookups, but he did have a girlfriend, once upon a time, and I wonder if that will ever happen again.

I return to my seat next to Jane and run my thumb over her wedding band.

I guess we'll just have to wait and see what the future brings.

About the Author

Jackie Lau decided she wanted to be a writer when she was in grade two, sometime between writing "The Heart That Got Lost" and "The Land of Shapes." She later studied engineering and worked as a geophysicist before turning to writing romance novels. Jackie lives in Toronto with her husband, and despite living in Canada her whole life, she hates winter. When she's not writing, she enjoys gelato, gourmet donuts, cooking, hiking, and reading on the balcony when it's raining.

To learn more and sign up for her newsletter,
visit jackielaubooks.com.

Also by Jackie Lau

Love, Lies, and Cherry Pie

Time Loops & Meet Cutes

Donut Fall in Love Series
Donut Fall in Love
The Stand-Up Groomsman

Weddings with the Moks Series
Four Weddings to Fall in Love
Three Reasons to Run
Two Friends in Marriage

Baldwin Village Series
One Bed for Christmas (prequel novella)
The Ultimate Pi Day Party
Ice Cream Lover
Man vs. Durian

Chu's Restaurant Series
The Sitcom Star
The Reluctant Heartthrob

Kwan Sisters/Fong Brothers Series
Grumpy Fake Boyfriend
Mr. Hotshot CEO
Pregnant by the Playboy
Bidding for the Bachelor

Cider Bar Sisters Series
Her Big City Neighbor
His Grumpy Childhood Friend
Her Pretend Christmas Date (novella)
The Professor Next Door
Her Favorite Rebound
Her Unexpected Roommate

Holidays with the Wongs Series
A Match Made for Thanksgiving
A Second Chance Road Trip for Christmas
A Fake Girlfriend for Chinese New Year
A Big Surprise for Valentine's Day

Chin-Williams Series
Not Another Family Wedding
He's Not My Boyfriend